2112

REVELATION

DEREK BEAUGARDE

Corkerhill Press

Published in 2024 by Corkerhill Press

Paperback: 978-1-7393929-4-9
eBook: 978-1-7393929-8-7

A CIP catalogue copy of this book can be found in the British Library and the National Library of Scotland.

Published with the help of Indie Authors World

Revelation 12:12 (New Testament and Psalms © The Gideon's International)

And had a wall great and high, and had twelve gates, and at the gates twelve angels, and names written thereon, which are the names of the twelve tribes of the children of Israel.

For my beloved grandsons Cailean and Lewis

Acknowledgments

The author wishes to acknowledge the valued assistance of Indie Authors World in the publishing of this book. The author also wishes to thank editor Gillian Murphy, reviewers Anita Dow and Andrew Marsh for their critical input. Also thanks to fellow alumni Sir Dirk Bogarde for the pseudonym and Allan Glen's School for the superb education. The author wishes to ascertain this is a work of fiction and any relation to any person living or dead is purely coincidental.

2112

REVELATION

**Derek Beaugarde's
stunning sequel to**

2084

THE END OF DAYS

BOOK 1: GENESIS

BOOK 2: EXODUS

BOOK 3: REVELATION

Prologue

On 26 May 2084 planet Earth was utterly destroyed. A rogue comet Schenkler HMM2, inadvertently discovered in 2081 travelling through the Kuiper Belt by Scottish astrophysicist Ewan Sinclair and computer scientist Gary Mackintosh, slammed destructively into the Pacific Ocean near the Marianas Trench.

The force of the impact from the huge comet cracked open the Earth's fragile crust like an egg, smashing its way through the mantle. The planet's molten core exploded in a huge cosmic fireball. Seven and a half billion humans were wiped out along with all other forms of life on the planet. The Moon and all its moon bases were also evaporated in the massive nuclear blast. All that now remained of Earth and its Moon was a swirling cloud of gas and space debris orbiting the Sun between Venus and Mars.

Due to the concerted efforts of the world's governing bodies, just over twenty-five thousand immigrants were successfully transported to the newly expanded Capitol Base settlement on Mars, aboard two huge fleets of Oceanus space-liners.

The Oceanus fleets also transported pre-fabricated infrastructure for the expansion of Capitol Base, including hi-rise buildings, factory equipment and sections of super-glass to build the city pods. It also included livestock and essential seed crops to allow for the continued survival of the human species. Furthermore, frozen stockpiles of human, flora, and fauna DNA from the late Dr. Marcie Venters' program were also transported to aid in the continued procreation of life on Mars. And, hopefully, one day out beyond the solar system into the Milky Way.

On that fateful final Oceanus LII flight, back in 2084, piloted by Space Commander Jack Crossan, travelled survivors,

Ewan Sinclair and Jill Geeson. Jill, who had not been originally scheduled to be on that fateful last flight from Earth, was pregnant with Ewan's child. That child was destined to become the 'first Martian'.

When the Oh LII was badly damaged by the shock waves from Earth's destructive death throes, many of the passengers and crew were killed or severely injured. Ewan suffered a severe head injury. He was kept in an induced coma for several days. While in recovery he and Jill agreed to be married. Jack Crossan performed the ceremony in his role as ship's captain.

However, the Oh LII continued to list powerlessly through the solar system. With the oxygen supplies leaking badly, the chances for survival of the remaining passengers and crew looked bleak. Fortunately, against the orders of Mars Control, Jack Crossan's former co-pilot Xi Xhu Pan, with Verne Andriessen and a small crew, had conducted a rescue mission on the Oceanus II. They reached the stricken Oh LII in the nick of time. All the surviving passengers and crew were transferred onto the Oh Two, except for Jack Crossan, who refused to leave his ship, along with a dying passenger. After watching the Oh Two head towards Mars, Jack turned his ship around. On dwindling oxygen and rocket fuel, Jack set the Oh LII back towards the Sun and the remains of the Earth gas cloud. He would never reach it alive.

Ewan and Jill made the remaining journey safely to Mars on the Oh II. They settled down to life in the giant super-glass pods in the newly-built city of Capitol Base. Their son Jack Crossan Sinclair was born at Marsdate 05:45 on 19 October 2084 Capitol Standard Time (CST), the first human child to be born on Mars. In early 2085 Jill was appointed as the chief news anchor at the newly formed CBTV station. It was not until late-2085 before Ewan could take up his role as Emeritus Professor of Astrophysics at the newly developing university of Capitol Base, or UCB. Being unaware at the time human population would stagnate, Ewan and Jill took the decision not to have any more children to concentrate on their careers.

Chapter 1

Marsdate: Tuesday 5 January 2112, CST, at half one in the afternoon. The dial showed a balmy -53ºC outside, warm for Mars. The newly constructed UCB Rover X rumbled its way over the rock-encrusted surface of the Red Planet. Twenty-seven-year-old geologist Jack Sinclair sat at the controls, guiding the vehicle through its final trials. Jack was nicknamed the first Martian, not a moniker he relished.

Born in October 2084 to parents Ewan Sinclair and Jill Geeson Sinclair, Jack arrived in the world shortly after they first arrived at Mar's Capitol Base. They had all survived the Armageddon back on Earth. Jill had only managed to get a place on the last Oceanus flight from Earth by sheer good fortune. On the perilous journey, she admitted to Ewan she was pregnant. Despite their fears, Jill gave birth to son Jack quite naturally at the Capitol Base Hospital. Jack was registered as the first human child born on Mars.

Jack spotted a large crater ahead. He turned to his assistant geologist Atlanta Caie, two years his junior, and winked.

"Okay, let's see how this baby copes with steep slopes?"

Jack revved the Rover and sped the vehicle onto the rocky upslope. The gears automatically adjusted for the steep climb. The huge tyres purposefully bit into the volcanic dust for greater stability. When the Rover reached the rim of the crater, the vehicle seemed to teeter momentarily on the edge, before starting to tip over onto the interior downslope. As it paused at the top, Jack pointed out of the cockpit windscreen to a spot in the far distance on the western horizon. Atlanta turned her head and squealed gleefully at the view.

"Oh my God, Jack. Olympus Mons – it's beautiful!"

"Yep, one day we need to go there."

Olympus Mons was the largest volcano on Mars. In fact, the largest known volcano in the solar system.

It was only now, after twenty-seven years of struggling for survival, that mankind had started to reintroduce manufacturing and technological processes once common back on Earth. This would allow scientists and explorers to travel out into the Martian hinterlands.

The Rover started on the crater's downslope. The back of the vehicle began to cant slightly to the left. The four-wheel-drive kicked in. Jack quickly straightened her up, making a controlled descent into the rock-strewn basin of the crater. At the centre of the crater, he brought the Rover to a halt, turning to his assistant.

"Okay, Atlanta, get the grabs out. Take a few test soil and rock samples. Who knows – as someone once sang, maybe there is life on Mars!"

To complement his joke, he turned on the music player. Jack selected the track of the old 20th-century rock star banging out his hit. Atlanta got to work delicately guiding the relevant exterior arms to scoop up some of the loose red sandy soil. She also grabbed at different sized rocks with the hydraulic pincers. Jack gave her a nod, indicating they had collected enough samples for this final test run of their new Rover.

"That's enough test running for today. The Rover's performed exceptionally well. Let's get back to Cee-Bee. Then we can start planning some real geological surveys."

Atlanta gave Jack the thumbs up. He was too busy concentrating on driving the Rover back up the inside of the steep red crater to spot her signal. She thought to herself, *all work and no play for Jack Sinclair.* Would he ever realise how deep her growing feelings were for him?

The vehicle bobbed over the rim of the crater. As it crawled back down to the Martian plain, they could see the distant lowering sun glinting off the domed surfaces of the huge super-glass pods back at Capitol Base, about twenty miles away. Jack revved up, driving back towards 'Cee-Bee' in virtual silence.

Chapter 2

Ewan Sinclair rapped his aluminium walking stick angrily against his study desk as he stumbled about awkwardly. He was frustrated at his lack of full mobility, on this his fifty-sixth birthday. Ewan had sustained some minor brain damage back in 2084 when the Oceanus LII was struck violently by the shock waves from the catastrophic Armageddon blast, which destroyed planet Earth.

His head injury had healed fairly quickly, but slight paralysis on his lower right side would remain with him permanently. He hated having to walk with a stick, particularly as he adjudged himself to be an otherwise fit youngish man in his prime.

Ewan sat down at his computer. He wondered where his wife Jill had disappeared off to, as he had not seen her for hours. They had both gone to the communion service at the St Andrew's Church earlier this morning. When they returned home, Jill said she had some shopping to do at the Cee-Bee Mall. Ewan had not seen her since then. He powered up his computer, ready to prepare his notes for an astrophysics lecture due this Wednesday at UCB.

The PC pinged out a message.

"New email."

Distracted from getting on with the job in hand, he opened up his inbox. His eyes boggled wide at the one new mail item in his inbox. It stated it was from Gary Mackintosh.

My God, he thought, that's impossible. Gary died back in 2084!

His best friend Gary was a computer whizz kid back then. Between them, they had made the startling discovery of the deadly Schenkler comet's passage through the Kuiper Belt in 2081. How can a dead man be sending an email twenty-eight years later? There was only one way to find out.

Ewan clicked the email open. There was a VMF video file and a JPEG file attached, but no typed message. Ewan opened up the video file. There on the screen was his old friend Gary's face as large as life. Ewan clicked the play button and Gary began speaking, which made Ewan's eyes well up with emotion.

"Well, well, well. If I'm talking to my old buddy Ewan twenty-eight years into the future, then I guess you survived to make it to Mars. Good for you! If that's the case then hopefully mankind still has a future too and that you and Jill are helping to procreate the fuckin' species. If I've got this right then today should be your fifty-sixth birthday, although I haven't a clue how you guys are working the Martian calendar up there. Anyway, a big happy birthday from your old pal – bet you never thought you'd hear from me again, eh?"

Ewan sat agog, listening to Gary as his friend continued, somewhat lowering his tone down to a secretive whisper.

"Ewan, I don't know if you remember all those years back in Houston when we were working with NASA? Probably not. But back then I told you that I had found something in NOAHSARK...."

Ewan recalled Gary's involvement with the NOAH-SARK project. The Network of All Human Specific Archives Research and Knowledge. It transferred a world-wide archive of data to the Martian MNET via the E2MSN. He could not remember anything about something secret Gary had found in NOAH-SARK.

"....something even I don't quite know what it all means. The only thing that I really know is that it's somehow the only archival material we input to NOAHSARK that someone or some group didn't want to be transferred to Mars. I found the data had been deleted twice and I thought it must have been a computer glitch. So I checked it and rechecked it. My conclusion always came back to one thing – human intervention...."

Ewan was puzzled by Gary's cloak and dagger approach. He started to wonder if this was just a hoax set up by his old friend for his birthday.

"....But they did not reckon on the great Gary Mackintosh.

Instead of re-inputting the data back into the standard indexed folder with the set library references, I've packaged it into this pre-set email to my old school pal Ewan Sinclair timed to arrive twenty-eight years into the future. I hoped whoever was trying to destroy the data would never think of that. Also, my theory was that if you weren't going to be around in 2112 living on Mars, then we, meaning mankind, probably didn't survive and the data wouldn't be seen by anyone. Jeez, it feels weird talking to someone in the future. Please tell me you're there old pal?"

Without thinking, Ewan replied aloud.

"Yes."

"Well for the sake of ma sanity I'm just going to assume you are. Anyway, back to the data. You should find an attached JPEG file, which has screeds and screeds of stuff on it, most of it's gobbledegook to me. Probably, it will be for you also. All I know is it has got something to do with Mars and it was important enough for someone to want it lost for all time. Well, old friend, I leave it all in your culpable hands. This is goodbye after all these years. Tell Jill I send her ma love and kisses. Oh and Ewan – happy birthday, old mate."

Ewan sat in stunned silence staring at the face of his old pal frozen at the end of the video play. He tried to fathom out how this could be transpiring after the passage of more than a quarter of a century. Only Gary Mackintosh could pull off a stunt like this, he thought.

Ewan motioned his index finger slowly towards the JPEG file on the screen. He was about to open it when he heard a muffled sound coming from the living room pod. Startled and unsure of who it might be, he quickly logged out of his email, closing his computer.

His right leg ached from sitting too long. He pushed himself upright with his walking stick, shuffling slowly to the door. Ewan stepped into the living room. He was taken aback at the group standing before him.

"HAPPY BIRTHDAY!"

Jill was standing in the middle of the room holding a large round cake. It looked like planet Earth with a large telescope rising from its centre surrounded by lit candles. His son Jack stood beside his mum, pulling funny faces at him. Jack's young assistant Atlanta Caie was also present, along with his retired astronaut friend Xi Xhu Pan, looking surprisingly old and frail. Plus a few colleagues from the astrophysics lab and the university.

In unison, they all began to badly sing 'Happy Birthday to You' quickly followed by 'For he's a jolly good fellow'.

Chapter 3

The first day back at the office for Elijah Gold after the Christmas and New Year holiday break did not exactly fill him with glee. Ah well, he mused, even the President of Mars has got to get back to work sometime.

He surveyed the papers in front of him on the desk. Gold thought of how this would be a big year ahead, a Presidential re-election year. It would be his last chance to run for a second term, four more years, based on the American political system.

His campaign team would be joining him at any moment. They would be eagerly awaiting his decision on whether he was standing down, or much more expectantly, he was running again for the Presidency. Over Christmas, Elijah had not thought about much else. In his mind's eye, he had pored over the trials and tribulations of his first four-year term.

The online tabloids, the 'Bloids', had been mercilessly panning his first term. Headlines screamed out at him such as 'President Turns Gold to Lead', 'Elijah: Prophet of Doom'. He felt the headlines did not do justice to his Presidency.

Elijah Gold felt he had guided the population on Mars through a period of peacefulness, relative stability, plus some, if not highly significant, technological progress. However, in general, the electorate, the press, Congress, even many in his party adjudged he had not achieved enough to warrant a second term.

The population of Capitol Base had become dissatisfied by the necessary long period of rationing of foodstuffs, commodities, and other scarce resources. They felt the government, led by Elijah Gold, had not done enough to progress the expansion of farming and agricultural super-pods. Furthermore, the development of industrial, manufacturing, technological super-pods had grown at a very slow pace. The Martian economy remained stagnant.

The population also remained stagnant, growing from

the original 26,000 colonists to over 36,000 in a quarter of a century. Even so, families were beginning to live in increasingly cramped and unsuitable living conditions.

Life expectancy had dropped to averages well below that previously achieved on Earth. Fertility levels were lower than expected. Infant mortality remained too high. With all the gloomy statistics in front of him, Elijah Gold wondered if it was time to hand the seal of the Presidential office onto some younger fresher political buck.

*

His door opened. Juanita Rossi, his loyal secretary, stuck her head in. Before she could say anything Gold spoke first.

"Is that the campaign mob ready to enter the lion's den?"

Juanita nodded her head.

"Oh, they're here alright, Mr. President. But the *Monseigneur* is outside. He's asked for a moment of your time before your meeting. Can he see you?"

The Monseigneur was what Juanita and Gold deprecatingly referred to when speaking about Cardinal Benedetto Cortopassi. Cortopassi, who arrived on Mars as a young novitiate priest, was currently the most senior cardinal below the Pope in the Roman Catholic Church. When he attained the priesthood, he was instrumental in reconstituting the Papal hierarchy on Mars. An ambitious man, he had aspirations to attain that high office himself one day. Gold could do without Cortopassi's intrusion today, but the Cardinal had always been a great help to his political ambitions.

Cortopassi had almost single-handedly delivered the Catholic vote to Gold four years ago, even though Gold was an agnostic. This was a key defining factor in his electoral success. A bit like the Mob delivering Chicago to an American Senator to win him the US Presidency back in the 20th century, Gold thought ruefully.

"Okay, Juanita, send him in."

However, before Juanita could even turn to inform the Cardinal, Cortopassi sailed on past the secretary, sliding into Gold's office. He must have been standing listening closely by the door. He barged past Juanita and over to the seated Gold, vigorously pumping the President's hand.

"Elijah, so good of you to see me at such short notice...."

Cortopassi then turned to Juanita and with a snort of dismissal he exhaled.

"....oh, and Juanita, it's Cardinal to you, not *Monseigneur!*"

Juanita Rossi glowered, swiftly spinning out of the office slamming the door, and Gold shrugged defensively.

"Please, Benny, Juanita means no harm. It's our private little joke."

"Hmm! From an agnostic like yourself, I can accept. That woman is a - a bloody Protestant. She tries to demean my position."

Gold shook his head.

"Let's not get into a religious argument. I'm sure that's not why you want to see me, is it, Benny?"

Cortopassi leaned closer to the President, lowering his voice.

"Of course not, Elijah. What I want to discuss is the spurious waste of money and resources on what I perceive to be useless scientific research."

Gold looked baffled and he shrugged at the Cardinal who continued his discourse.

"As you well know this city is struggling for lack of resources and technological developments in the fields of food production and fertility treatment...."

"Fertility treatment! I thought you Catholic guys were against that sort of thing?"

"The Catholic Church has always steadfastly maintained procreation should be a natural process. But we have to accept, that here on Mars, with a struggling population of less than forty thousand, we need scientific intervention to help kick-start regrowth."

"And get you more parishioners, Cardinal?"

Gold noticed Cortopassi's eyes narrow in reaction.

"Of course, Elijah, more parishioners mean more voters, one way or the other."

Elijah raised his palms to indicate the two should not get into an argument.

"Okay, point taken, Benny. I agree key resources and finances should be directed at food production and fertility. So what's this spurious scientific research that's draining these resources?"

"Geology!"

Gold was in the dark.

"Geology? What about it?"

"Well, Elijah, my sources at the university have informed me funding is being provided by the Congress to back a wasteful project of geological surveys out in the Martian hinterlands."

"I'm not fully up to speed with that one, Benny. But surely mankind has to find out what our new planet is made of. There might be lots of useful resources out in the hinterlands we can utilise?"

"Possibly so, Elijah, but d'you think at this critical juncture John Q Taxpayer wants to know the difference between one red rock and another? Or, whether he's going to be able to put a piece of red meat on his children's dinner plates?"

Gold noticed the digital clock on his desk ticking on. His campaign team would be champing at the bit.

"Okay, Benny, I take your point. Let me look into this for you and see what can be done. Okay?"

Cortopassi nodded and rose to quickly leave, turning his head as he reached the door.

"Thank you, Mr. President. That's all I ask for. Oh, and hopefully, we can look forward to working together for four more years!"

It seemed to Gold the Cardinal almost slithered out of his office. Gold buzzed Juanita to send in his election team. He quickly decided he would be advising his team 'four more years' was a goer. If only for Gold to keep the likes of Cortopassi in check.

Chapter 4

Ewan deemed his laptop at the Capitol Base University much more secure than his home computer. He waited a few days, until he had a quiet moment in his office, before examining the files Gary Mackintosh emailed him from back in 2084. He slipped his pen drive into the USB port, loading up the external drive with the folder, which he named GMAC2084. There were three old JPEG files, opening them up one by one. He squinted at the pictures, his face a portrait of puzzlement. They appeared to be photographs of old rock fragments. He wondered why Gary had been so damn secretive about these photographs. Why would anyone have gone to the trouble of erasing them from the NOAHSARK programme?

At first sight, the only key difference Ewan could detect, apart from the differing shapes, two of the rocks appeared to be of grey granite, whereas the third rock was a reddish-pink sandstone. Ewan pondered on the pictures, wondering if that told him anything?

Not really, he thought. Possibly the grey stones originated from one region of Earth and the reddish-pink one came from another part of his destroyed planet.

Maybe Jack, his geologist son, might be able to throw some light on their origins. Until Ewan had some sort of clue what he was dealing with, he decided it was not the right time to involve Jack.

Ewan looked at the time on his computer which showed 17:15. He had promised to take Jill and his son Jack out for a burger meal tonight at seven. Estimating he had about five minutes before he needed to head off home, Ewan replayed Gary's video to reveal any clues he may have missed. There was nothing concrete in what Gary had to say, except that he seemed convinced 'someone or some group' was determined to keep those photographs from being stored in the NOAHSARK programme. Ewan knew Gary would be adamant his pet project was trying to be sabotaged and not something Gary would make up.

However, he needed to leave.

Ewan was just about to shut down his laptop when Father Tomek Turkowski suddenly popped his head in the door. Ewan looked up startled. The university chaplain laughed at Ewan.

"What're you up to then? Have I caught you looking at something naughty, Ewan Sinclair?"

Before the professor could even attempt to shut down his laptop, Turkowski almost magically stood by his side. The cleric peered at the screen, examining the photographs still on show.

"Old rocks? What's all that about?"

Ewan stumbled around in his head, looking for an answer.

"Oh, umm, oh yeah, it's just some rocks my geologist son Jack emailed me to look at. He's been out testing his new Rover buggy thingymajig. His, eh, mechanical grabs picked these up as test samples. To be quite honest, they're a bit boring to look at if you ask me. Rocks aren't my thing. Give me stars any day."

"You're not wrong there, Ewan."

Ewan started logging out, quickly pocketing the pen drive.

"Anyway, Father, what d'you want me for?"

Father Turkowski shook his head and tutted.

"Ewan, you said you'd drop me off in your air-car at St Bartholomew's tonight for my meeting. You said it's on your way home?"

Ewan slapped his forehead.

"Sorry Father, of course, I did. You know - when I suffered that head trauma back in eighty-four on the way here to Mars - it left me with some slight memory defects. Anyway, that's me finished for tonight, so if you're ready, let's get going. I've got a date with a burger!"

Chapter 5

An hour later, twelve men, all attired in various ranks of the Catholic clergy, sat around a large circular table, which was in the centre of the badly lit basement of St Bartholomew's Chapel. They sat silently fiddling with their papers and notes as they awaited the Grand Master to begin the meeting.

The Grand Master, none other than Cardinal Cortopassi, let the eleven others sweat it out. The ambitious Cardinal determined to keep tight control over the group. After a tense silent moment or two, he spoke brusquely to them.

"I, Grand Master, bring this meeting of the Secret and Sacred Order of the Protettorato into order. May the Lord our God grant us His gracious protection. That we may also protect His most secret and sacred Seal of the Revelation."

The twelve men all bowed in prayer, chanting solemnly together.

"May the Lord our God grant the Protettorato His gracious protection. That we may also protect His most secret and sacred Seal of the Revelation."

They simultaneously picked up a small scalpel sitting in front of them. Each made a tiny incision in their right palm. Just enough to let a drop of blood start to seep out. Taking it in turn, each man shook the hand of the other on his right, letting their blood mingle. Blood brothers. Cortopassi waited while each man placed a small plaster on their palms to stop the blood flow. He then addressed the assembly.

"Brothers, I've called this special meeting of the Protettorato to discuss the single agenda item, which I've set before you. Let me read it out. *Item 1 – to discuss and agree on actions necessary to protect any incursion endangering the Seal of the Revelation.* Are we all agreed on this item?"

Before the group could agree, Father Tomek Turkowski interjected.

"Grand Master, I don't understand this item. I thought our forebears in the Protettorato back on Earth had ensured by their actions there should never be any threat to the Seal here on Mars?"

Cortopassi indignantly snapped back at Turkowski.

"Brother, I'm the eyes and ears of the Seal. In my opinion, I deem something new has emerged. If allowed to go ahead, it could theoretically endanger our ancient secret. Now – can we all get on and discuss this item?"

The other clerics all nodded. Cortopassi continued.

"Good. Now to the detail. It has come to my attention that a young scientist – a geologist – has been testing a new long-range research vehicle. It appears quite soon he intends to start actual geological surveys, heading out for the first time into the Martian hinterlands."

Father Robertus Algeo raised a hesitant, questioning hand.

"Master, you perceive that as some sort of threat? Surely the purpose of such a mission will be to identify useful mineral deposits, lands suitable for new settlements, extending farming, allowing for the regrowth of the human race. Isn't that what we all ultimately want?"

"Yes, of course, Robertus. I do want to see the populace on Mars multiply. It's a fact, is it not, we could argue larger numbers mean a larger Church of Rome. That's certainly one of my *own* ambitions. However...."

Cortopassi paused for effect.

"....at this juncture, I perceive a great danger in having this young man scrabbling around - God only knows where - on and under the surface of Mars. We can't afford for him to find something he isn't even looking for!"

Algeo raised another question.

"Do we even know whether he intends to survey in Cydonia?"

The Dominican Father David Balcanguel, dressed in the

habit of the Blackfriars, interjected angrily.

"Robertus, you know full well we don't speak of specifics of the Seal at these meetings. The walls have ears!"

Algeo lowered his head, glancing meekly across at the glowering Grand Master.

"Apologies, Master."

Cortopassi pursed his lips, forgiving the indiscretion with a nod.

"Robertus, watch your loose tongue. Back in the days of the Spanish Inquisition, it would have been cut out! But, getting back to your question. We don't know exactly which specific locations are being planned for geological surveys. Tomek, you're our eyes and ears in CBU. I want you to find out what you can about all the plans for this project?"

Turkowski nodded.

"Leave it in my hands, Master."

"Good. I've also recently spoken with President Elijah Gold on this matter. Without, of course, elaborating on my true concerns. I've sowed the seeds with him that Congress shouldn't be ploughing good money into such a fruitless project. If he goes for my proposal that should put a stop to it, or at least, slow it down to our advantage."

Algeo had another question.

"But, Master, what if Gold does not get re-elected later this year?"

"I've found the agnostic Gold to be quite a compliant President. This has been beneficial to our aims. We should, therefore, do everything in our power to ensure he gets re-elected."

Heads nodded in agreement. Then the Blackfriar Balcanguel spoke, stroking a ragged scar running down his cheek.

"Master, what if our efforts to slow down or stop the geology project by influencing the government has very little effect? What if we also find the survey does include those locations we'd certainly consider threatening to the Seal?"

Cortopassi's eyes narrowed. He scanned around the table like a snake searching for its prey.

"Then the Protettorato will have to employ all means fair or foul to protect our Lord's great secret."

There was a stunned silence. They knew how far the old Protettorato back on Earth had gone to protect the Seal. Some felt a fearful shiver run down their spines. Cortopassi broke the silence.

"Any questions before I break up the meeting with the benediction?"

Turkowski raised his hand.

"Grand Master, what's the name of this young geologist at the university?"

Cortopassi shuffled around in his notes.

"His name is Jack Sinclair."

Turkowski was taken aback.

"My God, I know of him. His father Professor Ewan Sinclair dropped me off on the way here tonight."

A sinister smile swept across Cortopassi's face.

"Excellent, Tomek. Then make it your mission to get to know the Sinclair family better. It may be to our advantage."

Turkowski felt something niggling at the back of his mind. The thought was lost to the moment as Cortopassi began the benediction.

Chapter 6

Jill, the anchor on *Good Morning Mars*, switched staring between the papers on her news-desk and the 3DTV remote-controlled camera facing her. The autocue would start rolling in one minute and she would deliver Friday morning's breakfast news to the Martian nation. It struck her the current audience share for her breakfast programme was barely 4,000. On a good day, if she was lucky.

Jill reminisced on her last day back on Earth, when she reported from the launch derrick of the last Jupiter Galaxy V shuttle to leave Earth. Her audience share was more like 5 billion tear-soaked beings that storm-filled day. Space Commander Jack Crossan's voice came flooding back to her. He screamed over the noise of the crashing thunder and the roar of the shuttle's booster rockets firing up.

"You're the only one here I see that's suited and booted. So get your ass in here and let's get the hell outta here!"

Jill's daydream was shattered, her focus back in the studio, as the director's countdown to broadcast infiltrated her thoughts. She quickly switched on her best TV anchor face.

"3-2-1. Jill on-air."

"Good morning, Mars. The time is 7 o'clock. I'm Jill Sinclair. This is your breakfast news for Friday 15 January 2112.

The headlines this morning.

In political news, President Elijah Gold is to announce later this morning he is running for the Democracy Party nomination for re-election to a second term in office.

In business and economic news, farming yields fall for the third year in a row. We ask, is the government doing enough to ensure our food stocks are being protected?

In legal news, the ultra-right Pro-Natural Life Party takes its case to the Mars Supreme Court to block the use of human DNA stockpiles from the Marcie Venters Memorial Hospital and Family Planning

Center.

In weather news, we hear more about the threat of a Martian hurricane with winds of up to 250 kilometres per hour heading towards the Capitol from our reporter, Barbara Mvula, on the half-hour.

These are your main headlines. We have much more coming up, including cooking tips from the Breakfast News chef Felicity McAdam and much more.

Stay with us and I'll be back after this short break."

The red 'Off Air' light shone. Jill relaxed, sorting her notes for the next airing of the broadcast. A young make-up artist came across and started retouching Jill's face. Jill sat back, closing her eyes. She drifted off into her subconscious. She thought back on how her life had changed so dramatically since 2084. Earth was no more. Her parents, family, and friends had all been evaporated from her life.

Here she was now, living in the glass bubbles of Capitol Base on Mars, married to Ewan, with her 28-year-old son Jack. She supposed in some ways their family had faired better than most. In some ways, Jill thought, survival for everyone was a constant daily struggle. The meagre human population of forty thousand was barely hanging on to existence on the Red Planet.

She could cope with the food rationing, the transportation difficulties around the city, the claustrophobia, and the stale recycled air pumped around the pods. However, it occurred to her, that at nearly 53, there was something else missing in her life.

"That's you all touched up, Jill."

The make-up artist's voice snapped Jill back into her anchor role. She waited for the auto-cue to begin rolling again. Just before the green light came back on, Jill wrote a mental note to herself. She would speak soon with Ewan about the issue troubling her. The 'On Air' light blinked on again and Jill got back to business.

"Good morning, Mars. Welcome back to your breakfast news with Jill Sinclair. The time is just coming up to 7:20.

Our main news this morning.

President Elijah Gold will announce later this morning he is running for the Democracy Party nomination for re-election to a second term in office.

It had been felt by certain political commentators President Gold had pontificated long and hard over this decision. Gold's popularity poll ratings have recently dipped quite dramatically.

For more on this announcement we go live to our political correspondent Misha al Rahman at the State House...."

Chapter 7

Later that Friday morning, Elijah Gold stepped back into the Oval Office with his key campaign strategists following on behind. A couple of minutes ago he had just finished delivering his nomination speech for re-election to the waiting press conference. He slumped down into his chair, addressing the team.

"Jesus H Christ! You know something, I don't even know if I want to do four more fucking years!"

They all voiced their disagreement with the President's statement. Campaign manager Barry Laverne spoke for the group.

"Look, Elijah, I know the polls are all looking pretty dire at the moment. On the upside, look at the contenders for the Conservatives. They're struggling to find a credible front-runner to stand against you."

Gold grudgingly agreed.

"I guess so, Barry. I'm just tired of working my ass off trying to get the human race back on track. Nothing seems to work in my favour."

"Elijah, it won't make much difference who's sitting in the Presidential chair. It's going to take centuries to recover from 2084. So we say – we're better off with the devil we know."

The others nodded and voiced their agreement. Gold waved them all to the door.

"Okay, okay! The lot of you clear off before I change my mind."

As the campaign team filed out, Juanita Rossi slipped past them.

"Mr. President, I've got that young man outside you wanted to see."

Slightly confused to whom Juanita referred, he glanced down at his schedule. He nodded, indicating Juanita should send him in. A minute later a flush-faced Jack Sinclair fumbled his way in past Juanita. Jack was in a state of disbelief as Gold pumped his hand, indicating to the young geologist to take a seat.

"Hmm, Jack Sinclair?"

"Ye-es, Mr. President?"

"Been hearing good things about you, Jack. I've heard all about your upcoming project. Planning to conduct geological surveys across the northern hemisphere – is that right?"

Jack relaxed a little, answering confidently.

"Yessir. My initial surveys hope to span out from Capitol Base as far as the lower slopes of Olympus Mons. At this stage that's the optimum range of the new UCB Rover X research vehicle. I wasn't aware you had taken such a keen interest in my research, sir?"

"You know, Jack – it pays for the President to know everything that's going on. The problem is, knowing what I know, can present its own issues."

"Why's that, Mr. President?"

Gold quickly glanced at his papers on his desktop then addressed Jack.

"Budgets, Jack, budgets. That's my problem. There just isn't enough cash to go around at the moment. At present the government coffers are cash-strapped. What with the need to ensure farming subsidies are protected and food production is maintained. The health service budget is a nightmare. In particular, fertility treatment is running way over budget. My job is to ensure sustainable population growth. Then I've got the goddamned ice-miners threatening to strike over their pay. Bastards have got my nuts over a barrel. We can't live on Mars without the water ice and frozen CO_2 these guys mine for us."

Gold let Jack mull over his pronouncement.

"I'm unsure what you're telling me, sir."

"Bottom line, Jack, is I'm going to have to curtail the government funding on the geological surveys for the foreseeable future. Certainly until after the upcoming election."

Jack was crestfallen. He had been working on the UCB

Rover X project for three years now. He now felt it had been all for nothing.

"But, Mr. President, my project could, in theory, be self-funding and a potential vote winner."

The phrase 'vote winner' touched a political nerve. Four more years, Gold mused.

"How so, Jack?"

"Well, sir, the main thrust of the project is to search for key metals and minerals. Production and technology are being held back due to a lack of metals like iron, copper, gold, silver, and zinc. Minerals like diamonds and quartz. For instance, a reasonably quick find of iron ore could probably have a working mine in production within a year. You'd be creating valuable new resources and much needed new jobs."

"Have we identified any iron here on Mars?"

"Well, we already know there is iron here on Mars. NOAHSARK documents Martian meteorites found on Earth, which suggests there is twice the amount of iron on the Martian crust than there was on Earth. Once significant deposits are identified it should be easier to mine, as there are no seas on Mars impeding sub-surface exploration. Initial mapping suggests volcanic deposits from Olympus Mons set down over millions of years across the Cydonian plain could potentially be mineral-rich."

Gold thought that Cortopassi would be fuming when he heard about his next decision.

"Here's the best I can do for you. I'll reduce your funding by fifty percent, rather than freeze it. If you come back with the mother lode – then the sky's the limit, Jack."

Jack thought about fighting for a bigger slice, but he guessed Gold was offering him his best deal.

"I'm going to have to trim my plans somewhat. But I'll take your deal, Mr. President."

Chapter 8

Ewan and Jill lay in bed exhausted bathed in warm, sweet perspiration after making love. Earlier in the evening, they ate a lovely dinner. They drank an exorbitantly priced bottle of wine, which had put them in the mood.

Alcohol production was severely curtailed by Martian law, as most arable lands were designated for food production. A basic bottle of wine cost a small fortune. They thought it was worth having this evening. Jill decided now was a good time to tell Ewan about that little niggle at the back of her mind.

"Ewan?"

Ewan was starting to feel post-coital drowsiness.

"Hmm?"

"How would you feel about me having a – a baby?"

Ewan was wide awake again.

"A baby! You're post-menopausal Jill."

"I know that. I'm still only in my fifties and otherwise reasonably healthy. I'm talking about having a baby by fertilised embryo implantation treatment down at the Marcie Venters Center."

"Wow, Jill, that's a big step. I thought we'd agreed back in 2084 to only have Jack and then concentrate on our careers? Jack's twenty-eight. How d'you think he'd feel about a wee brother or sister?"

"First things first. I want to know how you feel. Personally, I feel a strong urge to have a baby. I'd also like to do my bit in some small way to help repopulate the depleted human race."

Ewan mulled it over. A wry smile crossed his face.

"Well, maybe we could look further into it. Can we sleep on it and discuss the details in the morning over breakfast?"

Jill kissed him on the forehead beside his scar from 2084. As her lips brushed the ragged scar, she felt a wave of love for Ewan sweep over her.

Chapter 9

Cortopassi was raging. A Sunday morning and he had just finished conducting ten o'clock Mass in St Mark's Cathedral. He struggled out of his episcopal vestments, his anger compounding the fight.

"Help me get these blasted things off, Tomek!"

Turkowski tried helping, however, between the two of them, the Cardinal became more entangled in his scarlet cassock.

"Oh, leave it alone, Tomek. You're making things worse. It's that bastard Gold who's got me into this state! May God forgive me on a Sabbath?"

Cortopassi thought back to his midweek meeting with Gold, making him furious again. Turkowski saw the rising tide of ire in his Cardinal's face, which began to look the same colour as the red zucchetto on Cortopassi's skull.

"How has Gold made you so angry, Benny?"

"Because he's failed to put the blockers on that blasted Sinclair's rock-hunting fiasco! One way or another Gold will pay for going against me."

Turkowski shivered with fear. He knew Cortopassi capable of anything to achieve his ambitions – even – God forbid – assassination. The Cardinal finally straightened out his vestments and indicated for Turkowski to pour some wine. Cortopassi took a sip of the expensive merlot, pausing in thought.

"What about you, Tomek? What've you found out from Sinclair's father at the university?"

Turkowski stuttered unconvincingly.

"I – I – am sorry, Benny. B – But I've not had a chance to speak with Professor Sinclair as yet."

Cortopassi exploded with rage, spraying red wine in Turkowski's direction.

"What! Do you think your Grand Master had made a mere request? Interrogating the professor was an order! Do you understand me?"

"Y – Yes, Master. I'll get on to it right away."

Turkowski scrabbled around in his brain searching for some scrap of memory to placate the Cardinal. A thought resurfaced.

"There was something, Benny. I remember it from when I last met the professor in his office."

"And what's that?"

"Well, it may not be important. Sinclair was looking at photos of some rocks."

"ROCKS!"

"Well – yes, Benny – he said they were specimens collected by his son on a test geological run. I think that's what he said."

"What did they look like, Tomek? This could be crucial."

"I don't know for sure. Just some kind of flattish rock fragments. Sinclair quickly switched his laptop off before I could pay any real attention to them."

Cortopassi sat silently, mulling over what he had just heard. He took a deep gulp of wine. Then he spoke quietly and deliberately.

"Tomek, I'm disturbed by what you've told me. Somehow, I want you to get hold of those photos and any other materials related to it. Find out what you can about the plans for the geology mission – that's an order!"

"Yes, Benny – I mean, yes, Grand Master."

"My gut feeling is events are transpiring which threaten to reveal the existence of the Seal of the Revelation. Gold was a bit vague on the UCB Rover project. He suggested it could be heading into God's sacred territories, which we in the Protettorato must defend at all costs. It's time for me to speak with Balcanguel."

An image of the sinister Blackfriar's scarred face flashed through Turkowski's subconscious. For the second time that morning, he shivered with abject fear and dread.

Chapter 10

After lunch on Monday, Jack strode briskly over from the university's geology department to his father Ewan's office for some advice. He sat down facing his father who had been working on his laptop.

"I'm not happy, Dad. The President's slashed my budget funding in half. D'you think I should ask for another meeting with him to try and negotiate for more money?"

"I dunno, Jack. What's your gut feeling tell you?"

"Hmm, probably I'd be wasting my time. Originally Gold said he's going to cancel all my funding. However, I convinced him that, if the project could discover valuable minerals and metals, then it would more than pay for itself. Gold said if that's the case more funds would be forthcoming for further research."

Ewan nodded.

"Then, I'd accept the funds Gold's offered you now. Just make sure your project is an outstanding success."

"Yeah, I guess you're right, Dad. Well, I need to get back over to the geology department. The initial start-up phase begins on the first of next month. We've to drone out all the equipment, supplies, air tanks, food, and water to the various base camps between Cee-Bee and Uranius Patera to stock up for us to survive the trip. We'll be out on the Cydonian plain for the best part of a month."

Ewan's brow furrowed and he gave Jack his best, worried father's look.

"I don't want you and Atlanta to be taking any unnecessary risks out there, Jack. You're going to be hundreds of miles from human habitation and safety. It won't be easy to effect a rescue mission if required."

"Oh, Dad, we're not going to need any rescue mission. I've planned this project meticulously for years. Anyhow, Base

Control can send out a rescue drone within a few hours if need-ed."

"Yeah well, just you make sure you bring Atlanta back safe and sound. I kinda like that girl, you know."

Jack blushed a little.

"Yeah, well I kinda like her too, Dad."

Jack rose to leave and his father raised a hand to detain him.

"Jack, I've been meaning to run something past you."

Ewan explained a little about the background to receiving the photos of the three rock fragments, without disclosing it came from his old Earth friend Gary Mackintosh. He showed Jack the photos and asked for his professional opinion. Jack examined the photos for a minute or so.

"They look like fairly ordinary slabs of sandstone or arenite to me. Most likely from Earth. Although, I'd probably tell you more about their composition if I saw them in the flesh."

"They are likely to have been destroyed back in 2084."

"Let me zoom in and see if I can identify any of the specific sand crystals, quartz, or lithic fragments?"

As Jack zoomed in towards a higher definition he suddenly stopped.

"Look, Dad. Each of the slabs has scratchings or etchings on them. Can you see that?"

Ewan peered at the photos on his laptop.

"Wow! Yes, you're right Jack. I hadn't noticed that before. What d'you reckon it means?"

Jack laughed at his puzzled father's face.

"Jeez, Dad, I'm a geologist – I haven't a clue what it means. Although, I know a man who might, right here on campus."

"Who?"

"Remember your old pal Xi Xhu Pan?"

"Of course, he was at my birthday party."

"Well, his son Jai Zhu Pan is the renowned expert on

the archaeology of our old planet Earth. He's the man you want to talk to."

Ewan pondered on his son's words for a moment.

"Can Jai Zhu Pan be trusted?"

"Trusted? Is this some sorta big secret, Dad?"

"Well, son, let's just say, for the moment – I'd like to keep this between as few interested parties as possible. Certainly, until I know what I'm dealing with."

"Ooooo! Major intrigue! Anyway, you can trust Jai. I'd stake my life on it, Dad."

Chapter 11

Wim Wendtlander crashed open the door to his office making his assistant Ng U jump out of his skin. Wendtlander tossed the legal documents he had been carrying across the room, scattering papers across the floor. They had just arrived back from the Mars Supreme Court. The court found against the right-wing Pro-Natural Life Party's action to ban the use of human embryos being sperm banked at the Marcie Venters Center for the procreation of human life. Party leader Wendtlander was apoplectic.

"Try to calm down, Wim. You fought a strong case today in court. I think we did our best."

Wendtlander was still livid and kicked at some of the papers on the floor.

"Bastard judges! They weren't even listening to our arguments. I hope God strikes the lot of them down and they rot in hell!"

Ng U scrabbled around in his brain for some sort of placatory comment.

"Why don't we try appealing to Cortopassi again? If we got the Catholic Church back onside then it would certainly slow down the work at the Venters Center."

Wendtlander rolled his eyes.

"Fucking Catholic Church! Who da thought the Pope and his simpering cronies would've been all for artificial insemination and embryonic research. What an ironic turn up for the books that is. All they can think of is human repopulation and additional future paying parishioners."

His Vietnamese-born assistant persisted.

"It might not hurt to have one last shot at Cortopassi. He's much more radical than the laid-back pontiff. You might still be able to bend his ear. Remember, he's got one eye on being the next Pope."

Ng U noticed he struck a chord.

Wendtlander calmed down.

"Hmm, you might be right, Ng. If we could get Cortopassi onside then it would make a difference. I'll tell you this – if the Catholics don't come along with us, then the time has come for more direct action."

Ng U frowned.

"What d'you mean, Wim?"

"I mean we blow the Marcie Venters Center to kingdom come, that's what I mean!"

The young pacifist Vietnamese did not like the sound of that.

Chapter 12

Jai Zhu Pan had been busy marking preliminary exams for his archaeology class at the university. It had taken Ewan until Friday to get a meeting set up. The young Chinese tapped on Ewan's door and he was welcomed in with a broad Scots smile.

"Jai, so good to meet you. You know your father and I go back a long way. He saved my family's life back in 2084. I understand you know my son? How is Xi Xhu?"

The young man bowed his head in deference to the senior don.

"My father is reasonably well bodily, Professor Sinclair, although he's now in a care home. He has quite bad dementia. He thinks he's still back on Earth."

"I'm so sorry to hear about Xi. Although on the upside, I guess we'd all rather think we were back on Earth. By the way, less of the Professor. Call me Ewan."

Jai smiled and relaxed. They settled down to the crux of the meeting. Ewan explained again broadly, as he did with Jack, without mentioning Gary Mackintosh's cryptic message, how he had come across the photographs of the three rocks. He outlined Jack stated they looked like fairly ordinary sandstone or arenite rocks, probably from Earth. Jack also noticed some unusual scratchings on them.

Ewan produced them on his computer for Jai to examine. The young Chinese zoomed in and out, rotating the photographs this way and that way on the screen. He then turned to Ewan.

"Have you ever heard of the Rosetta Stone, Ewan?"

"Vaguely, I was never big on history."

"The Rosetta Stone was a granodiorite stele, found back on Earth in 1799, inscribed with three versions of a decree issued at Memphis in 196 BC on behalf of King Ptolemy V. The top and middle texts are in Ancient Egyptian using hieroglyphic and Demotic scripts respectively. The bottom is in Ancient Greek. As the decree has only minor differences between the three versions, the Rosetta Stone proved to be the key to deciphering Egyptian hieroglyphs."

"So, are you saying, Jai, these rocks are some kind of Rosetta Stone?"

Jai shrugged his shoulders a little.

"Hmm, I'm not sure. I'd need to research this further. The two light coloured sandstones, well, one looks like archaic Sumerian, maybe a bit more sophisticated in form. The second one looks like a more stylised form of Egyptian hieroglyphics. They're actually like nothing I've ever seen before."

"And what about the other stone, Jai?"

Jai shook his head.

"The darker red rock? To be quite honest, Ewan, it does look like writing. But it's of a form I've never seen before. Actually very sophisticated in form for something scratched on a rock."

Ewan mulled over the young archaeologist's words. He felt this must have something to do with what Gary Mackintosh encouraged Ewan to uncover.

"D'you think you can translate the rocks?"

Jai nodded.

"I think I could have a good crack at it. If you email me the photos, I'll get right on to it, Ewan."

Ewan panicked slightly.

"Um, look, Jai, presently I need to keep this tight for certain good reasons. I can't email it to you. It needs to stay safe on my computer for the present. Could we make arrangements for you to come to my office and work here on the transcriptions?"

Jai looked perplexed at all the secrecy. He agreed he would work on Ewan's computer starting on a couple of evenings next week. As they finished up their meeting Ewan thanked Jai for his valuable time. He put his forefinger to his lips.

"And, Jai, this is just between you and me for now."

Chapter 13

Father Tomek Turkowski had pretended to be working in the university library all Saturday afternoon. He was a regular visitor at UCB and would arouse no suspicion with the university security staff, who all knew him well. The library closed at 19.00 on Saturdays. Turkowski knew he now needed to make his move.

On the pretence of going to the men's room, he slipped unseen upstairs. He quickly moved towards the senior staff offices. It did not take him long before he stood outside Professor Sinclair's office. The door was locked but of a basic type. It did not take the priest long to use his trusty break-in tools to unlock the door.

Once in, he locked the door behind him. He knew he had to work quickly, in case security started to wonder where he was. He sat at Ewan's computer and powered it up. Ewan had not noticed the ever-inquisitive priest had watched as Ewan signed on, memorising his username.

All Turkowski needed now was to get past Ewan's password and he was in. He was an adept hacker. Something Cortopassi had used to devious effect in keeping tabs on his rival cardinals, the pontiff himself, and even unbeknown, to other members of the Protettorato.

It only took around ten minutes to crack the password and hack in. Five more minutes, all that was required to find the folder named GMAC2084, holding the files he desperately sought. The folder contained the JPEGs showing the photographs he had previously seen. Turkowski also noticed a VMF video file in the same folder.

Might as well copy the whole folder for Cortopassi, he thought.

Aware time was marching, he swiftly transferred the folder and files onto his memory stick, logging out of Ewan's computer. After switching the computer and lights off, he stepped back out into the corridor, rattling the door handle to ensure it was locked.

Just as he moved to return to the library he was stopped in his tracks by a strident voice behind him.

"Father Turkowski?"

The priest spun swiftly around to see security officer Joe Jaap, who had just appeared around the corner. Turkowski tried to retain a veneer of calmness.

"Joe, hi there, doing the last rounds?"

"Sure am, Father, be glad to get home soon. But what's ya doing up here on a Saturday?"

Turkowski kept it light.

"You know, Joe, I was just trying to see if Professor Sinclair was in today doing some research work. I'd found something on astrophysics in the library I wanted to run by him, but...."

Turkowski rattled the locked door handle for effect.

"....looks like I'm out of luck, Joe."

Joe Jaap gave the priest a dubious look.

"Never known the professor in on Saturdays. I think he likes his weekends too much. I like mine too, so why don't we start making a move for home, eh, Father?"

"Good idea, Joe. I'll try and pop in next week and catch the good professor then."

Chapter 14

On the following Monday, Ewan flew his air-car from his suburban pod to the UCB air-car park. Still too early for students to be arriving and the place was quiet.

As he strode across the air-car park he noticed the bulky figure of one of the security guards about a hundred metres away talking to a swarthy looking man in a hooded cloak. The guard was unmistakably the affable Joe Jaap. Ewan could not make out the other man.

"Bang!"

A loud crack shattered the air. Joe Jaap crumpled to his knees, then toppled forward. Transfixed, Ewan screamed.

"Joe!"

As he dashed towards the stricken guard, the hooded man sprinted away. Other security staff came running out of the main university block. Ewan tried to help turn Joe's bulky body around to provide first aid. It was immediately obvious poor Joe was stone dead.

He had taken a single bullet right between his eyes. Blood and brain matter oozed out the gaping hole in the back of his head onto the ground. One of the other guards shouted to Ewan.

"What in hell's happened here?"

Ewan stumbled for words.

"I – I don't know really. I just saw Joe talking to a tall hooded man when I arrived and the next thing I heard him getting shot. Why'd anyone want to shoot Joe?"

"Dunno, Professor, we've called an ambulance and police. They should be here any minute. Jeez, Prof, poor old Joe. Wouldn't ah hurt a fly. Poor guy was due to retire in the summer."

Within a few minutes, an ambulance arrived followed by three police cars with their sirens blazing. Ewan and the other guards staggered back. They watched as the medics and cops buzzed around the lifeless body of Joe Jaap.

The area was quickly cordoned off and turned into a crime scene. A forensic tent was erected around the dead guard's body as students and other staff began arriving on campus. A small concerned crowd started forming around the cordon. Nothing like this had ever happened before at UCB buzzed the crowd.

Ewan and the other guards, attending the scene, were taken into the main block to be questioned. The hapless Ewan was the only witness to the killing, while the others, on hearing the gunshot, had run out to find Ewan bending over Joe's body. None of the guards saw the tall, swarthy man in the black hooded cloak Ewan alleged had been the perpetrator of the crime.

However, at this stage, the detectives taking the statements noticed Ewan was pretty shaken up by the events. They briefly recorded what their one and only witness had to report. Once the interview was concluded, the lead detective advised Ewan he would be required down at police HQ for further questioning. Ewan was then allowed to carry on with his day.

The Rector took Ewan into his office and arranged for hot sweet coffee to be brought. They spent about twenty minutes talking about the dreadful event. Once the Rector was assured Ewan had calmed down, and he would take the rest of the day off, he allowed Ewan to carry on.

"I'm just going up to my office to email my wife Jill and let her know what's happened. Then I'll head off home."

The Rector nodded.

"Well, make sure you go home after that. You're too shocked to do any work today. Ewan, let me know if you need some time off to get your head straight?"

Ewan went directly to his office to email Jill. Although he knew she would still be finishing off her breakfast news broadcast on CBTV. Jill's phone would be off. He quickly powered up his laptop and logged in. As soon as his home page opened there was a pop-up appeared onscreen.

"UCB SecureGuard software detected unusual login activity on this device. This device may have been the subject of an attempted hacking incursion. You should immediately change your password to keep this device secure."

My God, he thought, *can this day get any worse for me? First, I see poor old Joe Jaap murdered in front of my eyes. Now it looks like someone was on my computer at the weekend. What could anyone want on this computer?*

Then it struck Ewan.

"Gary's files!"

He quickly checked folder GMAC2084. The files were still intact. He was relieved about that, but he had no way of knowing whether the hack had been successful, or whether those files were what the hacker was after. It occurred to him a rogue student may have been seeking to find astrophysics test papers or exam results. Ewan decided it was highly unlikely.

Ewan thought to himself Gary Mackintosh's files were the only plausible source of information a hacker would be after. The problem was he had only shown the files to two others; his son Jack and Jack's archaeology friend Jai.

He trusted his son Jack implicitly. He had no reason to think he would try and hack into his own father's university laptop. However, he had only met Jai for that one meeting. At this juncture, Ewan could only imagine Jai was the only plausible suspect for the hack on Saturday.

Maybe the Chinese archaeologist had seen more than he had let on when he viewed the rock scratchings. Maybe he wanted the files for his exclusive personal research. Although, Ewan remembered Jack stated he would stake his life on Jai's trustworthiness.

Ewan thought that maybe Joe Jaap's murder in the aircar park earlier on had rattled his brain so much that he was suspicious of everyone and anyone. From his meeting with Jai, the young fellow professor came across as a straight-up guy.

Even so, Ewan felt he could no longer risk having the

GMAC2084 folder on his university laptop. He removed the folder and files to a memory stick to take back home with him. He would get Jai to do the rock photos research there in the evenings after work.

He quickly emailed Jill about this morning's terrible events. It struck him Jill was likely to have been reporting the emerging news story on her *Good Morning Mars* programme. For Ewan, it had certainly not been a good morning on Mars for him. A pang of emotion stabbed his saddened heart.

Oh, to be back on sweet Mother Earth, he opined.

He headed back out of the main campus block, walking past the crime scene tent, surrounded by busy forensic officers clad in their white overalls, caps, and overshoes. He did not hang about and headed straight for the UCB air-car park.

Chapter 15

Cardinal Benedetto Cortopassi sat at his laptop, with Father Tomek Turkowski sitting nervously beside him, as they pored over the contents of the GMAC2084 folder. Cortopassi initially loaded Gary's video file and they listened intently. The Cardinal, with tightly-knitted brows, took salient notes.

"Ewan....remember....Houston....working with NASA.... found something in NOAHSARK....something....don't quite know what....means....archival material....input to NOAHSARK....some group didn't want....transferred to Mars....packaged it into....email to....Ewan Sinclair....to arrive twenty-eight years....into future.... find....JPEG file....most of it....gobbledegook....something to do with Mars....important....want it lost for all time."

Turkowski turned to his Grand Master and shrugged his shoulders.

"There's nothing of any substance in this video. This friend of Sinclair's – this Gary Mackintosh – hadn't a clue as to what this material's about. Surely we've nothing to worry about, Master?"

Cortopassi was not as circumspect.

"Hmm, Mackintosh knew some things which concern me. He knew the files he kept uploading to NOAHSARK had great importance. Also, some group – meaning us – wanted the files deleted and kept secret. And he worked out the information had something to do with Mars."

"But, Benedetto, surely it would take Sinclair a great leap of ingenuity to connect what he's found to the Protettorato and the Seal of the Revelation?"

Cortopassi flashed an irritated glance at his underling.

"Sinclair's an intelligent and resourceful man. We must make sure he never makes that great leap of ingenuity. Let me look at the JPEG files."

The Cardinal opened up the JPEGs. He stared at the

photos as if staring into the eyes of his nemesis.

"God in heaven!"

Turkowski watched the colour drain from Cortopassi's face and he was perplexed. He looked at the photos, the same ones he had previously snatched a glance at when visiting Ewan. He could not begin to fathom why they had his Grand Master looking like death warmed up. They looked like three fairly ordinary rocks.

"What's wrong?"

Cortopassi snapped back.

"I'll tell you what's wrong! What we're looking at is one of the greatest secrets of the Protettorato. These rocks are passed down from one Grand Master to his successor along with the secrets of their purpose."

"Are you saying you have these rocks here on Mars, Master?"

Cortopassi nodded, ominously lowering his voice.

"I do, but, if I told you where, I'd have to kill you. You see these rocks are the keys to unlocking the Seal of the Revelation."

Just then, there was a light tap on Cortopassi's office door. The sinister Blackfriar Balcanguel slithered snake-like into the room. Cortopassi and Turkowski looked up sharply from the screen at their Protettorato comrade. Balcanguel removed the black hood from his head and spoke in a hissing whisper.

"The deed is done, Grand Master."

Cortopassi nodded with a show of satisfaction. Turkowski was puzzled.

"Deed – what deed?

Cortopassi quickly explained.

"When you called me on Saturday evening to let me know you successfully obtained the Mackintosh files, I asked you if anyone saw you that might have raised suspicion. You mentioned the security guard Jaap found you at Sinclair's door."

Tomek Turkowski glanced at Balcanguel and noticed an

evil sneer cross over his face. The priest's stomach flipped over and he felt rising bile.

"Yes, Benny, I'm sure he had no idea I had been in the professor's room."

"You might be sure, Tomek, but it's my sacred role as Grand Master to be doubly sure. The Seal must be protected at all costs. Unfortunately, that protection means, sometimes a sacrifice becomes necessary."

This time Turkowski's colour drained from his face.

"Y - You don't mean Joe Jaap?"

Turkowski listened incredulously as Cortopassi spoke with an air of ironic false sympathy.

"Unfortunate, although necessary. The poor man was due to retire soon, which greatly saddens me. Balcanguel also feels deep remorse at having to carry out such a grim task. He's asked me to take his confession later. Jaap was a Catholic too. I'll speak with the pontiff and make sure the Vatican takes care of the unfortunate man's funeral and financial arrangements are put in place for his dear widow."

The priest felt sick to his stomach and asked to be excused. Cortopassi, with resolute omnipotence, declined. He explained matter-of-factly the three of them had important work remaining to discuss. What was now required to be done with Ewan and Jack Sinclair?

Chapter 16

Later that afternoon, Kurt Reich was shown into Elijah Gold's office by Juanita Rossi. Reich was the Chief of Police for Capitol Base. The President had summoned him to discuss the shooting on the UCB campus. Murders on sparsely populated Mars were reasonably rare. Although, when they did occur it was certainly unusual enough to warrant the President's attention.

There were always two or three murders a year out in the poorer eastern pods, usually gangland feuds, drugs or domestic violence. Further out on the remote Martian icefields, it was also expected to see a couple of homicides annually. Mainly ice miners, violently falling out after too much cheap moonshine or gambling disputes.

A homicide on the affluent campus at UCB, in the city centre pod, not far from the State buildings and the seat of government, was a different proposition. Practically unheard of and something Elijah Gold felt he needed to get a handle on. Especially, when running for four more years. A quick resolution to this crime would certainly not dent Gold's chance of re-election.

"So, Kurt, what do we know about this poor guy Jaap's killing?"

Reich brought Gold up to speed.

"Joseph Jaap. A sixty-two-year-old security officer at UCB campus. He'd worked there for going on twenty years and due to retire early in the summer. Well-liked. No known enemies or anyone who held a grudge against him. Fatally shot in the head in the air-car park on campus at around 08.10 this morning. It appears he was shot with his own weapon. The gun and bullet have been recovered and are in forensics for testing."

Gold interjected.

"His own gun you say? Could he have shot himself?"

Reich continued with his report.

"We've not ruled suicide out at this stage, Mr. President,

but it's unlikely. Jaap was a happy-go-lucky individual with no financial, marital, or health issues. On the flip side, we do have a witness who stated he saw Jaap talking to a tall hooded man in the air-car park. That witness alleges he heard the shot. He then saw the assailant running off as Jaap dropped dead. So it does appear to be a homicide. Although, at this stage, we've no credible motive for the killing and no other witnesses. Unfortunately, a CCTV blind spot. So we've no video footage on campus to work with."

Gold continued questioning.

"This witness. Who is he? Is he a suspect in any way?"

Reich turned a page in his folder and carried on.

"Ewan Sinclair. Emeritus Professor in Astrophysics at UCB. On the face of it, he's a respectable citizen. No criminal record. Highly respected at the university. He was just arriving for work as normal when the shooting took place. At the moment, sir, there is little reason to suspect Sinclair, however, we only have his word this alleged hooded man was the killer. The other security staff ran out to find Sinclair bending over Jaap's body. None of them saw any hooded man running away. Forensics are checking the gun and Jaap's body for any evidence that may implicate Sinclair in the murder. You know, sir, fingerprints, DNA, the usual stuff."

A thought occurred to the President.

"Hmm, you said this professor was called Sinclair. Would he be related in any way to Jack Sinclair, a young geologist at UCB?"

Reich scanned his notes.

"Funnily enough, sir, Jack Sinclair is Professor Sinclair's son. Does it mean anything to the investigation?"

"Probably not, Kurt, but young Sinclair is about to conduct geological surveys out into the Cydonian hinterland. I've rubber-stamped Congressional funding for the project. I even had some strenuous objections to the project from some quarters. Sinclair convinced me there could be significant material and financial returns on investment if the surveys were successful. Although I'm kinda rambling off base, Kurt. This has probably nothing to do with your investigation."

Reich had been scribbling some notes down.

"I dunno, sir, at present we don't have any specific motive for the killing. Money is always a massive motivator when it comes to murder. It sounds like there could be significant assets involved with this project. I've got to keep an open mind on any kind of lead. Can you say who the objector was in the case of the geological project, Mr. President?"

Gold pondered on Reich's question for a moment.

"Sorry, Kurt, at present I'm not prepared to give you a name. All I'll say is that it's someone fairly high up in the Catholic Church – and, no, it isn't the Holy Father himself. However, if you found some evidence linking Joe Jaap's murder, which I'd doubt, to Jack Sinclair's project, then don't hesitate to come back and discuss this. I'm keen we resolve this case quickly and cleanly. I believe we're both running for re-election this year, so it isn't a good time to be upsetting the voters with an unsolved murder in the heart of Cee-Bee city. Is it, Kurt?"

The Chief of Police caught the President's drift. He scribbled 'high up Catholic' in his notes. Reich excused himself to return to CBPD HQ and get back to the case.

Chapter 17

Jill had rushed back home as soon as she finished up the debrief meeting after her *Good Morning Mars* broadcast. She spent the rest of the day catching up with the terrible events Ewan had been embroiled in on the campus. She fussed over her distraught husband. She met Joe Jaap on a couple of occasions and Jill was quite upset to have heard of his untimely death.

Always the professional newshound, Jill had asked Ewan to tell her everything. He related what he could remember about Joe's murder and of the tall hooded man.

"I'm sorry, Jill, there's not a lot more I can add. It all happened so fast."

Jill could tell Ewan was still in shock. She wondered if his old head injury impaired his powers of recall.

Ewan went on to relate to Jill about the hacking incursion on his office computer. He had not discussed the message from the past from their old school friend Gary Mackintosh with Jill.

"I hadn't wanted to broadcast it too widely until I had unlocked the meaning of the rock photos."

Jill was understandably miffed.

"Ewan Sinclair, I've never known you to keep any secrets from me throughout our married life. So – even Jack knew about this before me!"

Ewan hung his head shamefully.

"I'm sorry Jill. From Gary's video, I'd the impression the people who tried to destroy this info might go to any lengths to protect their secrets. I only involved Jack for his professional knowledge. He also recommended his archaeology colleague Jai Zhu Pan. After the hack, I now fear I may have told one too many about the rock photos."

Jill shook her head.

"I'd seriously doubt Jai would try to hack into your computer, not if he's like his father, Ewan. I'm sure Jack wouldn't have recommended someone he couldn't trust himself."

"I agree, Jill. Although there is no-one else who has seen those rock photos...."

Ewan stopped himself in mid-sentence. *Unless,* he questioned ruefully, *but surely not?*

Jill was about to ask him what he was thinking. They were interrupted by their son Jack arriving to comfort his dad. Ewan complained he had had enough of people fussing around him. Although deep down he respected the love being shown by his wife and son.

He discussed the hacking with Jack. Ewan's son was adamant Jai could be fully trusted. He was sure his Chinese friend would not be involved in such an act.

"I'm glad to hear that, Jack, because I've arranged for Jai to come here tomorrow evening to work on the rock photos."

Jack's eyebrow arched with interest.

"Hey, Dad, okay if I come over too? This rock thing is getting more intriguing by the minute. Maybe I can throw my tuppence worth in from a geological perspective."

Jill laughed at her son.

"No show without Punch then. So I guess that's dinner for four?"

Ewan agreed Jack could join the meeting the following evening, then shooed his son off back to work. Jack was happy to shoot off. They were making final preparations for the drone transfers of supplies and equipment to go out to the various campsites to be set up between Cee-Bee and the Cydonian plain. Jack explained he and Atlanta planned to leave on the UCB Rover X in four weeks to begin the geological surveys in the shadow of Olympus Mons.

Jill groaned.

"Oh God, now I've got my son and his lovely assistant to worry about, on top of what's happening to my husband."

As Jack rushed out the door he laughed back.

"Don't fret, Mum. Atlanta and I have planned this trip down to the nth degree. Nothing'll go wrong."

After Jack left, Ewan reassured Jill their son knew exactly what he was doing and that everything would work out fine. Jill said it was a mother's job to worry about her children.

On that note, Jill said she had something else on her mind she needed to discuss. Jill explained she had been to the Marcie Venters Center. She had an appointment the following week to be assessed for embryo implantation to have a post-menstrual pregnancy.

Ewan listened intently to his wife's hopes and fears concerning the appointment. He assured her she was still as fit and healthy as a woman half her age. If anyone was going to be successful, then Jill was. Ewan finished off with a laugh.

"After getting on to me. Who's been keeping secrets from who then, Mrs. Sinclair?"

Chapter 18

The two men had never met before. Although each knew of the other very well. The meeting was in a secret location in the eastern suburbs, the poorer pods. They both detected the fetid staleness of the recycled air, heavily polluted from the nearby industrial plants. Cortopassi and Wendtlander eyed each other up. Both knew they were men formed out of the same rotten mould. Full of cunning and dangerous ambition. After initial pleasantries, Cortopassi got down to business.

"Well, Mr. Wendtlander, what pressing matter has brought me to you in such a stinking hole of a place?"

Wendtlander went on to summarise the series of cases his Pro-Natural Life Party had brought before the courts leading up to the Supreme Court. The action had been raised to block the embryology and fertility work of the Marcie Venters Center but was dismissed by the city's highest judges.

Wendtlander knew Cortopassi would have been fully briefed on the cases, however, he went through the motions. The Cardinal listened impassively, before replying.

"I'm sure you're aware the position of the Catholic Church has, by necessity, changed since its reconstitution on Mars. Our Holy Father has stated the Church has no objections to the work carried out by the Marcie Venters Center. Our key concern is population growth on Mars has remained stagnant and fertility levels are worryingly low. The Holy Father's doctrine lays down Catholics should take all steps necessary to increase procreation."

Wendtlander bent forward with narrowing eyes towards Cortopassi.

"That's the Holy Father's doctrine, Cardinal. What would your doctrine be if *you* were Pope?"

"Quite frankly, Wim, I'm ambivalent on the issue. And as I'm not *il Papa,* and I'm only one Cardinal amongst many, I'm afraid my views one way or the other would have little sway on the Vatican."

The Pro-Life leader hesitated for a moment and then pressed on.

"Yes, but my dear Cortopassi, if you were to be Pope...."

Cortopassi interjected angrily.

"Look, Wendtlander, the Holy Father is still in his early sixties. He could be Pope for another twenty or so years, so I feel we may be wasting each other's time here. So it's immaterial whether I could be swayed by your Pro-Life argument."

"But, Cardinal, what if the Pope was unfortunate enough to have a short tenure? You're surely odds on to be the next Holy Father."

Cortopassi was slightly unnerved by what he had just heard. Unnerved, but intrigued.

"What are you suggesting, Wim?"

When the Cardinal left thirty minutes later, he could not believe he had just agreed with the leader of the PNLP on how to eliminate the Holy Father and slow up the work of the Marcie Venters Center in one fell swoop. However, as he drove back towards the Capitol pod, he took some satisfaction in knowing he was one step closer to his greatest ambition.

He would be the next Pope.

This would put him in a more powerful position politically. He would have greater sway with Elijah Gold. This would also elevate the standing of his organisation, the Protettorato, and the influence it could exert on the Catholic Church. Most importantly, he could use his increased powers as Pope to curtail the work of that young geologist Jack Sinclair. This would ensure the secrets of the Seal of the Revelation remained locked away for eternity.

Chapter 19

After dinner with Jill on Tuesday evening, Ewan ushered Jai and his son Jack into his study. At dinner, they had discussed the awful shooting of Joe Jaap on their campus. Jai had said he had been shocked when he heard the news on Sunday morning's breakfast news. He had been tied up at an important archaeology conference all day Saturday across town in the Cee-Bee Conference Center. Jai had been oblivious to the tragedy unfolding at the university.

Ewan pondered that Jai would certainly not have been in his office on Saturday. It could not have been the young Chinese who had hacked into his laptop. Jack had read his father's thoughts and gave him a secretive knowing wink across the dinner table. It still nagged at Ewan as to who else could have wanted to hack his computer. Maybe, it *was* just an errant student looking for examination papers or test results.

In the study, the three men quickly got down to business. Ewan loaded up the photographs of the flat rock fragments. He zoomed down to a level where the markings were as legible as possible for Jai to read.

The archaeologist did not recognise and could not translate the unknown markings on the reddish rock. He decided to concentrate on the archaic Sumerian and Egyptian hieroglyphs. Ewan printed out various blown up photos for Jai to work on. Jai moved over to Ewan's workstation to interpret the various markings. Jack and Ewan continued to pore over the photos on the laptop.

A thought occurred to Jack.

"Dad, these look like very high-res photos. How much can you zoom in on them?"

"Dunno, Jack, we can try 100 times magnification if you want?"

Ewan zoomed in on the two similar light-coloured rock

photos. The markings became obscure, however, the structure of the rocks remained very distinct. Jack nodded sagely.

"Hmm, they're both very similar in their geomorphology. They're similar to rocks that would have been found in the deserts of south-west Jordan, in thick sequences of continental sandstone of the Cumbrian-Ordovician age. Also found in the Sahara Desert. Great blocks of these sandstones were used in the building of Sumerian tombs and the Great Pyramids of the Pharaohs in Egypt."

"Wow, well spotted, Jack. So these rock fragments may have been preserved inside ancient tombs?"

"Looks like it, Dad. Maybe that's why the markings have remained intact after thousands of years. Can you try the same magnification on the other rock?"

Ewan zoomed in on the reddish rock and let his son study it. Jack looked at the photo quizzically and asked if Ewan could try it at 1000x magnification. Amazingly, the resolution remained sharp, like looking at the rock through a microscope. Jack shook his head.

"This can't be right?"

Ewan asked Jack what the problem was.

"If I'm right, Dad, this looks like a fragment of butte or mesa-forming stratified rock from the Western Arabia Terra region."

"Ah, so a lot further south than the Jordanian desert then?"

"No, Dad, the Western Arabia Terra region is on the boundary of the Meridiani Planum. Right here on Mars!"

Ewan was stunned.

"Mars! So are you saying it's part of a meteorite?"

"This was no meteorite, Dad. There is no evidence of any thermal reaction with the oxygen-rich atmosphere of Earth which burns up a meteor into a meteorite. This rock looks like it was just picked up from the Martian surface as if it had been yesterday."

"How the hell would a pristine Martian rock with carvings on it have been on Earth along with ancient rock carvings created thousands of years ago?"

Jack shrugged his shoulders as Ewan struggled for an answer. Something jogged in Ewan's memory. He fast-forwarded to a point on Gary Mackintosh's video and set it to play.

"*....Something to do with Mars and it was important enough for someone to want it lost for all time....*"

Ewan visibly gulped.

"My God, Jack, I think we're starting to stumble onto something here. Something certain people on Mars want to make sure remains secret."

"Yeah, but what, Dad?"

"At this juncture, I've no idea!"

Jai, who had been working studiously in the background on translating the photos, suddenly interrupted the conversation.

"Maybe I can help a little, guys."

The young Chinese archaeologist explained the rock fragments in Sumerian and Egyptian were, almost certainly, translations of each other. Although he had not identified the other language, it was likely to be a similar transcript, just like the Rosetta Stone allowed archaeologists back on Earth to decipher from Ancient Greek to unlock the secrets of Egyptian hieroglyphs. Ewan was impressed.

"So, Jai, are you able to say what the carvings on the rocks tell us?"

"Well, they kinda read like this. *The last of the great beings of the red traveller sowed his seed among the beings of the blue traveller. Many seeds failed. One seed thrived and then there was the new being.*"

Jack raised his hands in complete puzzlement.

"Very biblical, Jai, but what does it mean?"

"Not too sure myself, Jack. I'm guessing the red traveller refers to Mars and the blue traveller is most likely Earth. So, something to do with a connection between Mars and Earth, I guess."

The three men sat silently not quite knowing what to say. Suddenly, they were startled, as Jill popped her head in.

"Hey, you guys! Have you seen the time? You've all got work in the morning to go to and I've got to get up early for my *Good Morning Mars* shift. So let's call it a night, eh? Oh, and Ewan. Remember, I've got my appointment at Marcie Venters tomorrow afternoon."

Chapter 20

Jill arrived just before one o'clock in the foyer of the Marcie Venters Center for her one-thirty appointment. Moments before, she had struggled through a large crowd of Papal supporters and PNLP protestors baying at each other and separated by a police cordon.

I picked the wrong day for my appointment, Jill groaned to herself.

In the foyer, she caught sight of her colleague Barbara Mvula with her cameraman. Jill headed over to have a quick word.

"So, Babs, I guess you're here to interview someone important. How d'you know I was going to be here today?"

Barbara began to splutter out a reply. Jill held up her hand laughing.

"I'm only kidding, Babs. I'd be a poor journalist if I didn't know the Holy Father was visiting today."

Barbara smiled broadly and replied.

"Yes, Jill, he'll be here about two. I hope to try and get a few words out of him."

As Jill waved goodbye to head for her appointment, she cheerfully shouted back to her colleague.

"Good luck with the interview. What a turn up for the books, Babs? Can you imagine a Pope visiting a place like this back on Earth?"

As Barbara was only twenty-three and born on Mars, she thought to herself, it would be hard for her to imagine. She knew what Jill meant, in terms of the significant U-turn in the ethical stance of the Catholic Church.

*

At one-thirty sharp, Jill was ushered in to meet her embryologist, Dr. Eva Schuster. Jill passed her the consent form signed by Ewan and Jill. The doctor gave a detailed explanation of the procedure for the implantation of the fertilised embryo Jill was to carry. Dr. Schuster also outlined all the risks inherent with such a procedure. Particularly, that only about one in three fertilised embryos survived to full term. Also, Jill's age was, to a certain extent, an inherent risk factor.

"However, Jill, as your doctor I'm delighted with your levels of fitness. Your body age is that of a woman of about thirty-eight. This is a definite plus factor."

Jill listened carefully to all the risks and benefits. After full consideration, she agreed with Dr. Schuster they should go ahead with the implantation procedure.

*

Meanwhile, down in the foyer, Barbara Mvula interviewed senior Catholic figures and other arriving dignitaries. She was able to catch a quick word with Father Robertus Algeo, part of the Pope's advance party.

"Father Algeo, thank you for talking with us this afternoon. In terms of the Holy Father's visit to the Marcie Venters Center, how significant would you say it was?"

"Glad to be able to talk with you, Barbara. I feel it is a highly significant moment in the history of the Catholic Church. It marks a sea change in our ethical and moral standpoint. It recognises embryology and fertility clinics now play an important role in the future survival of the human race."

"And Father, what would you say to the protestors outside from the PNLP who vigorously oppose human intervention in the natural order of procreation?"

"Well, Barbara, of course, I've great empathy with their arguments. It was also the Catholic Church's stance back on Earth before 2084. However, God's guiding hand has changed things dramatically since then. The human race has gone from eight billion, back on our beloved blue planet, to less than forty thousand here on Mars. A planet so hostile to human habitation, we are struggling to multiply and procreate. We believe we have to do everything in our power to give mankind a chance to survive. The Marcie Venters Center has its part to play in that ultimate goal."

Barbara Mvula thanked Father Algeo as he moved off to continue preparations for the Holy Father's arrival. Then she waved Ng U of the PNLP towards her and her cameraman. The young Viet had been allowed in by security to represent the alternate side of the argument.

"Ng U, assistant general secretary of the PNLP, thanks for joining us this afternoon. Can you outline to our viewers why you have mounted a large protest against the visit of the Pope to the Center today?"

"Thanks for having me, Barbara. Our protest isn't specifically aimed at the Pope himself. However, he does represent high profile support for what we'd fervently argue are unnatural and unethical procedures. As such, it allows the PNLP to present our critical arguments to a mass audience."

"Surely, Ng U, that's the point Father Algeo made just a few minutes ago on behalf of the Catholic Church. We do *not* have masses of people. He argued, we've gone from eight billion back on Earth to less than forty thousand here on Mars. Without the work here at the Center, population growth is expected to continue stagnating. How would you counter that argument?"

"I'd counter it by saying, His Holiness is more concerned about falling rolls of communicants in the Catholic Church and less about the natural order of procreation God conferred to mankind through Adam and Eve. Life always finds a way and humans should stop tinkering with Mother Nature."

"Just before you go, Ng U, can you tell us why your leader Wim Wendtlander has decided to stay away from today's protest?"

"Well, Barbara, Mr. Wendtlander had fully prepared

to lead our peaceful protest today. Unfortunately, he's received some very serious death threats on social media over the past few days. It was deemed better he stayed away, rather than risk his own life...."

Ng U added sarcastically.

"....I'm sure the Holy Father wouldn't want to risk losing a single person's life – not even Mr. Wendtlander's!"

The young Viet concluded the interview with a sarcastic sneer. After leaving Barbara Mvula he headed back outside to join the main PNLP protest.

*

Upstairs on the second floor, Dr. Schuster came into the recovery room where Jill had been resting, following the implantation procedure. The embryologist checked Jill's pulse and temperature and gave her heart a quick listen on an old-fashioned stethoscope. Then she nodded.

"Well, Jill, all is looking good."

Jill was surprised at the short time required for the procedure.

"Is that it, doctor?"

"That's all there is to it, Jill. Now, all we do is wait and see if nature takes its course. You're free to leave whenever you're ready."

A few minutes later Jill strode downstairs. She was startled as someone came rushing past her, also heading downward. As the man turned quickly on the landing he glanced furtively up at Jill, flustered and perspiring. While he rushed on ahead, Jill realised she knew him from past interviews on *Good Morning Mars*. Wim Wendtlander.

She briefly wondered what bothered him, but then went back to dreaming of the possibility of new life growing within her womb. Jill continued downstairs and started along the ground floor corridor towards the main foyer.

Suddenly, she froze as she heard angry shouting and a commotion just around the corner in the foyer.

*

Outside, Wendtlander had arranged for Ng U to start an organised pitched battle with the unsuspecting Catholic crowd, to coincide with the Pope's arrival in the foyer. Wendtlander knew this would deflect the police and Center security staff to deal with the disturbance outside.

Wendtlander strode purposefully into the foyer, as Barbara Mvula commenced her interview with the Pope. The PNLP leader quickly drew out a gun. His loud cry stopped everyone in their tracks.

"Death to the Holy Father! Natural life to the unborn!"

He fired three bullets in quick succession. Before anyone could react, he triggered an IED bomb strapped to his body, followed by a blinding flash and a crashing explosion. Bodies and glass were blown in all directions.

Jill, still standing around the corner in the corridor, thrown backward by the shockwave of the blast. Outside, the battling crowd came to a sudden halt as glass and smoke billowed out of the front of the Center.

Ng U suddenly realised the enormity of the situation. His boss Wendtlander had set him and the other PNLP supporters up for his devious criminal intentions. As Ng U and others were being quickly arrested, he could only think of two short words.

"Oh, shit!"

Chapter 21

Jill's eyes flickered open to meet the glare of the overhead lights and curtains surrounding her. She quickly realised she was in a hospital bed. As she squinted her eyes, the concerned faces of her husband Ewan and son Jack came into focus. They smiled to see her regain consciousness. Jill was puzzled.

"Wh - what happened?"

Ewan pressed her hand lovingly.

"There was a bomb went off in the Marcie Venters Center and the blast knocked you out. The doctors kept you in mild sedation to allow your recovery. This is the first time you have woken up."

Jill, although still groggy, went naturally into newshound mode.

"A bomb at Marcie Venters? But who? Why?"

Ewan would rather have held back, however, he knew his wife's journalistic instincts would have pushed him for the story.

"Well, it's all still a bit vague, Jill, and the police are still investigating. Reports are stating the explosion was carried out by a suicide bomber. They're saying it was Wim Wendtlander of the PNLP, although it has not been confirmed."

Jill's eyes widened.

"My God, Ewan, he ran past me seconds before the explosion. But – why?"

It was Jack who filled the pregnant pause.

"Mum, again it's unconfirmed. The rumours flying around are that the target was the Pope. It doesn't sound hopeful the Holy Father has survived."

Jill choked back emotion.

"Oh Jeez, that's awful, but…."

Ewan interjected.

"But nothing, Mrs. Sinclair. Just you forget about sniffing about as a newshound for the present. Your job is to get your-self better and that's an order!"

Another pregnant pause. Then Jill addressed the ele-phant in the room.

"What about the embryo? Is it okay?"

Ewan patted his wife's hand.

"The doctors say it's too early to say if the embryo was damaged in the blast. Let's just take one step at a time and let's get you better."

Jack agreed.

"Yeah, I want to make sure I've got a mother to look for-ward to. Then I can worry about whether I have a new wee broth-er or sister on the way. Oh yeah, and when were you two going to tell me about that little secret?"

Chapter 22

Black smoke billowed from the New Vatican's chimney. The pontiff was indeed dead. Killed in the blast at the Marcie Venters Center, where seven had died, including the Pope, Wendtlander, Barbara Mvula, and her cameraman.

The cardinals had been called into closed session. As they sat silently praying for their dead Holy Father, Cardinal Benedetto Cortopassi was the first to stand before the red-clothed assembly.

"Holy brother cardinals. This is indeed one of the blackest days in the history of our Mother Church. Our esteemed Holy Father, only the second pontiff on Mars, so cruelly cut down in his prime by the wicked terrorist Wendtlander. Brothers, we must make arrangements for the funeral mass and the pontiff's internment here in the New Vatican."

Cortopassi, hawk-like, scanned the cardinals and watched as they nodded reverentially before he continued speaking.

"It's never a good time to discuss the succession of a new pontiff. Especially so, when our Holy Father has been vilely assassinated. The Holy Roman Catholic Church must prevail. It must be led strongly, ardently, and with piety into the future. With that in mind, I'm informing this court of cardinals my full intention to stand for election. I would hope I can count on your support and certainly look forward to serving our Mother Church as its new Pope."

The hawkish eyes once again surveyed the room, trying to gauge the level of support. Cortopassi knew he could count on the cardinals who were sympathetic to the Protettorato. He also knew he would not receive the votes of the softer, younger cardinals with their modern Martian outlook on the Church.

He opined that he did not perceive too many dissenting faces. His chest puffed out with the pleasant thought he would soon be the head of the New Vatican. This would give him even more power over his Martian flock and even more influence in Martian politics. It further crossed his mind, the sooner the better, to stop the meddling research exploration out into the Martian hinterlands by that young geologist Sinclair.

Father Tomek Turkowski reported that Sinclair's expedition was still due to leave next week. This was despite the geologist's mother being caught in the blast at the Marcie Venters Center. A prayer to God flashed through Cortopassi's mind, seeking forgiveness for any injuries to innocent bystanders caught up in the blast, including Jill Sinclair. Cortopassi had no idea she was to be there on that fateful day, but God-willing, that lily-livered ineffectual Pope had to be eliminated.

Chapter 23

Early morning on Monday 15 February 2112, a small invited crowd of dignitaries gathered at the Western Gate, the main air-lock for entering and exiting Capitol Base on its western extremity. They were seated on a small grandstand temporarily erected for the departure ceremony on the edge of a cornfield. The ceremony was arranged to celebrate the commencement of the UCB Rover X Geological Survey.

Jack and Atlanta were itching to get started. They had to listen to the boring oratory being spouted by the Dean of Geology at UCB. They snatched odd phrases like 'humankind's historic mission' and 'advancement in the geological and scientific knowledge of the Red Planet'. They raised their eyebrows in exasperation at each other. As their eyes met, both felt their hearts skip a beat.

My God, I've never seen Atlanta look so beautiful.

The thought took him by surprise. He was snapped out of his reverie by a ripple of clapping from the small gathering.

Jack rose and gave a short and sweet response to the small crowd, including his parents. He invited Atlanta to 'suit up'. They both clambered into the cockpit of the Rover to the sound of rapturous applause. They both waved cheerily to their audience and Jack could see his parents wiping proud tears away. Control radioed to the Rover that the inner gate was open. Jack steered the vehicle into the large air-lock. Jack and Atlanta glanced at each other as they heard the inner gate lock. They waited for the signal the outer air-lock was open. Atlanta spoke first.

"Well, Jack, here we go on our big adventure."

"Yep, Atlanta, it's Olympus Mons or bust."

"Well, at least Uranius Patera or bust, Jack."

They felt the outside pressure drop as the outer gate slid open. Jack revved the Rover into action. With a last look back through the red-dusted glass of the Western Gate pod, they could just make out the grainy figures of the crowd. The Rover gained traction and pulled out onto the sandy Martian foothills of the Western Arabia Terra.

Both wondered, with some trepidation, what lay ahead of them in the undiscovered lands to the west in the Cydonian Plains and the towering Uranius Patera volcano, about thirty kilometres short of Olympus Mons. As the air-lock closed behind them, they drove forward to Base Camp I, where they would spend their first night on the hostile Martian surface.

Red dust devils rose and swirled close to the vehicle. Jack and Atlanta prayed these nasty little devils did not develop into a full-blown Martian sandstorm.

Chapter 24

Later that Monday morning, in the New Vatican's Chapel Superior in St Peter's Cathedral, the Martian equivalent of the Sistine Chapel, the twenty-four gathered cardinals, two attendant doctors, and housekeeping staff, heard the keys turn in the locks. They began with a prayer for the success of the Conclave to elect a new Pope.

The prayer was led by Cardinal Josiah Nbekele, the chosen Camerlengo, the Pope's chamberlain. It was his task to oversee the election process.

"O Holy Lord in heaven and our beloved Mother Maria. Look down on this Conclave gathered here in holy session. Bless us with your omnipotent wisdom. Your eternal truth. Bring us together as one united holy catholic brethren. Show us the true path. Allow us to faithfully elect our new leader here on Mars. Let us all affirm before God and the Cross, all that should pass within the confines of this Conclave, remain secret for all eternity. This do we affirm?"

The whole gathering murmured their affirmation.

Cardinal Benedetto Cortopassi, head bowed reverently in prayer, slowly surveyed through his slit-eyes, the other scarlet-robed peers seated around the table prepared for the Conclave. He knew he required to get two-thirds of the vote. Sixteen of the twenty-four cardinals needed to be in his favour, to be elected Pope. The process could go on for days, however, Cortopassi desperately sought a swift and successful conclusion to the vote.

*

He had angrily watched the departure of Sinclair's Rover trundle out towards the western hinterland on *Good Morning Mars*. He knew it was imperative to get the election over as quickly as possible. This would allow the Protettorato to meet to finalise a strategy to ensure the protection of the Seal of the Revelation.

Every day locked in the chapel, a day lost. It was another day bringing Jack Sinclair dangerously close to unearthing the secret the Protettorato had kept for almost two thousand years.

Previously, it had been kept by an underground sect of Hebrew Pharisees. It was believed the scrolls had been handed down from the time of Joseph. The scrolls had been copied from the Pharaoh's Great Library of Alexandria, then brought out of Egypt by the followers of Moses.

*

The cardinal knew he had to exude an air of unhurried calm as if he had all the time in the world, but he desperately wanted the Conclave over and done with. Camerlengo Nbekele interrupted Cortopassi's train of thought.

"We now come to that stage in the proceedings where we place the nominations on the table in front of us. In each case, I'll ask for a seconder. As you all know, Cardinal Cortopassi has already announced his intention to stand for election as Pope. Can I ask for a seconder?"

Cardinal John O'Carroll, a lower order member of the Protettorato, who had been well primed in advance by Cortopassi, raised his hand.

"Seconded."

The Camerlengo added this to the minute and continued.

"Cardinal Benedetto Cortopassi is duly nominated to stand for election. I'll now ask if any other cardinals wish to be nominated. Is there anyone else who wishes to throw their mitre into the ring?"

There was a polite ripple of laughter and then a moment of silence. Hmm, this might just be a formality for me, thought Cortopassi. Then the silence was quickly broken.

"I'd like to nominate Cardinal Pietro Malvoli."

"Seconded."

The Camerlengo again noted this and looked around the table again.

"I nominate Cardinal Alexander MacEachen."

"I too second."

After placing this third nomination in the minutes, the Camerlengo raised his head, quickly spotting a look of frustrated ire on Cortopassi's reddening face.

"Cardinals, it would appear we've got an election on our hands. I propose we cast an initial vote. If a clear winner has gained the required two-thirds majority, then we can quickly proceed to light the white smoke, signifying we have a new Pope. If there is no clear winner we will break for lunch. In the afternoon, each nominee will give a formal presentation to the Conclave on how they intend to lead our Holy Mother Church under their papal tenure. Is that agreed?"

"Aye."

Ten minutes later the Camerlengo was ready to give the results of the secret ballot.

"Cardinals, I have the results of the first ballot. Cortopassi – ten votes. Malvoli – eight votes and MacEachen – six votes. Therefore, being that there is no clear winner, I suggest we break for lunch, and then we will listen to the three candidates' presentations thereafter."

The Camerlengo walked across the chapel to make arrangements for lunch with the housekeeping staff. Cortopassi was less frustrated, after noting he led the first round of voting. He was unconcerned about addressing the Cardinals with some great oratory in the afternoon.

Instead, he prepared to play politics during lunch to gain the six votes required to become Pope. He needed to try and weed out the six cardinals who had voted for MacEachen. If he could swing them then he could snatch the crown from the closest candidate, Malvoli.

After lunch, the three candidates gave their presentations on their aims and aspirations for the Papacy. Cortopassi readily admitted the other two had given much better orations than his own, particularly Malvoli, whose stirring modernising speech soared above the other two.

However, Cortopassi had busied himself around the lunch tables. He was sure he could count on most of the traditionalist MacEachen's support, certain he had turned around at least a couple of the MacEachen cohort. The Camerlengo called for the second round of voting. After another ten minutes, he was in a position to announce the result of the second ballot.

"Cardinals, I now have the results of the second ballot. Cortopassi – fifteen votes. Malvoli – nine votes and MacEachen – no votes. I, therefore, announce Cardinal MacEachen is withdrawn from the voting process. Cardinals, with your agreement, following a break for tea and coffee, we will have further presentations from Cardinals Cortopassi and Malvoli."

Cortopassi was annoyed the process was being drawn out for another round of voting, given that he was only one vote short. He would work his charms on Camerlengo Nbekele, who he knew to be in the Malvolian camp. If he could tempt Nbekele with a suitable promotion within the Vatican, it would swing the vote in his favour.

Cortopassi's thoughts were interrupted when Cardinal Malvoli rose to speak to the gathering.

"Cardinals, my holy brothers, it's quite clear to me in what direction the voting is going. Rather than us wasting more time on another round of voting, I offer to swing my vote to Cardinal Cortopassi and give him the required two-thirds majority."

The Camerlengo addressed the Cardinals.

"Cardinals, do we all say aye to Cardinal Malvoli's proposition?"

Outside the New Vatican, a crowd of about two thousand worshippers milled around, although, no one expected a quick result. Suddenly, one parishioner looked up and cried out with joy.

The excited crowd could see the white smoke rising from the New Vatican's chimney.

"Look! We've got a new Pope!"

Chapter 25

Elijah Gold sat across his Oval Office desk from Cortopassi – now the elected Pope Benedict I of Mars. The President cracked a smile and joked, half in earnest.

"Well, Holy Father, am I still allowed to call you Benny?"

Deep down Cortopassi was miffed. He grinned back without betraying any emotion.

"Of course, Elijah, we go back some ways now. I hope we will always remain friends."

Gold nodded affirmatively, without giving any vocal confirmation to Cortopassi, and then continued impassively.

"Well, Benny, of course, my congratulations are fully extended to you on being elected to the highest office in your Mother Church. I know it's not the way you'd have wanted the office, following in the 'dead men's shoes' of your unfortunate predecessor. However, I know you hoped to be *il Papa* one day."

Cortopassi nodded vigorously.

"Of course, of course, Elijah. Such a tragedy. I wrestled with my conscience for many days, after that evil pig Wendtlander's suicide bomb took away our Holy Father, before being urged by many of our Cardinals to step into the breach."

"I'm sure it's an easy decision in the end for you. Anyway, you asked to see me, Benny, so how can I help?"

Cortopassi cleared his throat.

"Ahem! Two matters to discuss with you, Elijah. Firstly, I know you aren't a church-going person. So I don't want to cause either of us any embarrassment. I wanted to ask you in person if you and your lovely wife would honour me with your presence at my papal inauguration in three weeks. My office will be sending out formal invitations, but I'd rather spare you having to turn it down on agnostic grounds."

Gold waved a conciliatory palm, dismissing such an

idea.

"Benny, don't be silly, of course, my wife and I will be there at the New Vatican. Wouldn't look good for an incumbent President to fail to turn up to a new Pope's inauguration, would it?"

Cortopassi laughed, with false relief, although, deep down, he knew that Gold would not miss a great photo-op in an election year, agnostic or not.

"And I sincerely hope I'll have the opportunity to be at your inauguration next January for your second term of office, Eli? I think you can count on me to get the Catholic vote out for you in the coming election."

Gold winced, ever so slightly. Only his wife and very close friends called him Eli. It looked as if Cortopassi's promotion to the highest office afforded him delusions of familiarity. Gold bit his tongue. He knew the new Pope elect was coming to the crunch.

"So, Benny, I think you said you'd two matters to discuss."

"Yes, yes, Mr. President, indeed. The other matter concerns this reckless and costly venture the young geologist Sinclair has embarked on. You gave me the impression you'd give it serious consideration to put a stop to this unnecessary financial burden placed on the Capitol Base taxpayers."

A pregnant pause ensued before Gold addressed Cortopassi.

"I gave it my consideration, Benny. Yes, I considered the burden on Cee-Bee's John Q Taxpayers. To that end, I seriously curtailed Rover X's Congressional budget. However, after being briefed on the project by young Sinclair, I found the investment returns on potentially expected mineral finds could heavily outweigh tax burdens."

"As you state, Elijah, just potential mineral finds. We don't know what's out there or where it might be. Meanwhile, as Sinclair and his assistant proceed with their wild goose chase, the city has to find new money from somewhere to repair the damage to the Marcie Venters Center. Reproduction, which is vital to mankind's survival, may have been set back years by that dreadful terrorist bombing."

Gold was now getting exasperated. He felt the need to wind the meeting up before it ended in a serious disagreement between the President and the Pope elect.

"Look, Benny, we know half the planet is covered in the red dust with a high ferrous oxide content. What we don't know is where the mother lodes of iron ore lie. The Sinclair kid is the planet's top geologist. His investigations and experiments have led him to conclude there are large deposits of iron ore out on the Cydonian Plain. As President, I feel the Rover X project is a calculated risk worth taking."

Another pregnant pause.

"For God's sake, Benny, what is it you have against Sinclair anyway?"

Cortopassi mulled the question over, searching for a politically correct reply. He needed to keep his cards close to his hand.

"Maybe, Elijah, I'm not a risk-taker like you. Maybe I just don't think the time is right to gamble away our scarce resources. Looking for, dare I joke, the Pot of Gold at the end of the rainbow. If you won't recall the Rover X project and save those costs, then I think we should leave it there. I mean to say, you're a busy man. You *do* have an election campaign to run too, you know."

As Cortopassi stood to leave, he made an almost imperceptive sign of the cross with his right hand towards Gold. The President wondered if the Holy Father had just made him a threat or a promise.

Chapter 26

A minute or two after Cortopassi left through Juanita Rossi's reception office, she buzzed through to the President as instructed. Gold strode over to the side door, opened it sharply, and beckoned the person standing there into the Oval Office. Once they were seated Gold spoke first.

"Well, what did you make of that? I take it you caught it all on CCTV?"

Kurt Reich, the Cee-Bee Chief of Police, nodded.

"Yep, Mr. President, I caught it all loud and clear."

"Well, what's your impression, Kurt, what d'you think is going on?"

Reich placed a case file on the desk in front of Gold and opened it up.

"Based on what I just heard there a few minutes ago, to be fair, the Holy Father did not give too much away. He was very careful with his words. There's no doubt in my mind he wants that project stopped. Maybe – at any cost."

"That's my impression too, Kurt, but why? This could have major benefits to Cee-Bee if Sinclair is successful. Why would Cortopassi want to stop that?"

Reich swept his gaze down at the file.

"Honestly, Mr. President, at this stage I've no idea. What I do know is this. Police investigations have been continuing into the murder of Joe Jaap at UCB campus. The outright conclusion is, young Sinclair's father, Professor Sinclair isn't complicit in the shooting. Sinclair's assertion he saw a hooded man commit Jaap's murder appears to be true."

Gold whistled softly and Kurt Reich continued.

"Jaap was deliberately shot in a blind spot at UCB. No hooded man was seen coming onto campus, nor one leaving. So it appears to be a planned hit."

"Is there a motive?"

"At this stage, we have not established any firm motive for a contract killing. My best guess is, Jaap was silenced because he knew something. Maybe even something he didn't even realise he knew about."

"So we're stumped then, Kurt?"

"Well, not completely. We got a break by spreading our search through CCTV footage city-wide. Ball-busting work, but my team spotted a hooded man entering into the UCB pod through its eastern airlock, which is about a mile from the university itself."

"Okay, where does that lead us?"

"Well, sir, the footage does not identify the suspect. His hood hides his face well. We followed a trail back to see what route the hooded man may have taken. Again, a ball-breaker for my guys, but worth it. CCTV footage picked up the suspect at various points, leading back to a specific start locus."

Gold caught his breath and allowed Reich to go on.

"That location was the Friary of St John in the Upper East pod. One of the poorest districts in Cee-Bee. Here, we got a break. The hooded man had just come out of the Friary and he stepped over to a stationary limo air-car. He dropped his hood to speak to someone sitting in the back seat. We have been able to identify him as Blackfriar David Balcanguel. We strongly suspect he killed Joe Jaap, for reasons unknown."

"Jesus, Kurt, some cleric from the Upper East has bumped off a decent, hard-working security guard at UCB for no apparent reason. Where the hell are we going with this?"

Kurt Reich flipped over a page, more for effect, as he had already prepared carefully what he would say next.

"There's more, Mr. President. We got the plates on CCTV and the limo air-car is registered to a Dyrk van den Bogaerde."

"Dyrk van den Bogaerde? Who in hell is he?"

"Well, no-one we suspect really. He's a professional chauffeur. Registered as a New Vatican staff member. More importantly, on that particular day, he chauffeured for Cardinal

Benedetto Cortopassi."

This time Gold whistled out loud and clear.

Chapter 27

Atlanta, in the driving seat, pointed out through the toughened-glass windscreen of the Rover, to let a half-dozing Jack observe the temporary dome of Base Camp III. Less than a kilometre ahead. She radioed in a SitRep to the control room back in Cee-Bee. Control acknowledged their appreciation the project was currently on time and schedule. She threw Jack a slow-mo fist bump. Atlanta felt the silent thrill of electricity surge through her body. It was the first time they had skin to skin contact since leaving the city five days ago. Neither could escape the emotionally-charged atmosphere in the cockpit. A tired, but excited, Jack spoke croakily.

"A great day's driving there, Atlanta. Some pretty tough terrain you had to negotiate, but - beautiful."

He hesitated before adding *beautiful*. Jack hoped Atlanta would assume he meant her driving skills. What he meant was the woman working alongside was so beautiful. He was beginning to fall big time for her.

The Rover's journey from Capitol Base had been spectacular in scenic terms, however, otherwise uneventful. Capitol Base was constructed from a site originally a NASA experimental station founded in 2045. It was rapidly expanded between 2081 and 2084, to accommodate the fleet of Oceanus space-liners bringing in the last vestiges of mankind, following the Schenkler HMM2 apocalypse.

The city sat in the foothills of the Western Highlands, which lay about 30 kilometres east of Cee-Bee.

*

Day one, Monday 15 February, the journey was a rerun of the route Jack and Atlanta had practiced a few times during the Rover's testing sessions. The vehicle performed beautifully.

Jack drove that day. The route was fairly straightforward. Mostly downhill into the red-dusted Western Arabia Terra region. Jack had one or two reasonably sized craters to skirt around en route. The dust devils they spotted on departure came to nothing. It had been a beautiful sunny day, although the Martian sunlight was never as strong as back on Earth. They reached the temporary pod at Base Camp I just before sunset. The outside temperature was -43°C.

They suited up, making sure each other's boots, helmets, and visors were all firmly fastened. Their surface suits had the thermal inner layers activated. They ensured their sleeve-mounted control panels were fully functioning. After they went through their final procedural checklist, they logged a call to Cee-Bee control. Then they transferred from the Rover, and in through the tight squeeze of the airlock of the temporary camp pod.

Although the pods were tiny, they were fully stocked with enough food, drink, air supplies, and other vital equipment to service them for the outward and return journeys. They also contained an abundant stock of lithium batteries to replenish depleted or faulty batteries on the Rover. Although the vehicle had inbuilt solar panels, to help recharge the batteries during the day, the rugged terrain of Western Arabia Terra took its toll. They needed to know fresh batteries were available at each base camp en route.

The first day, after the adrenalin rush of their formal send-off from Cee-Bee, had zonked the pair. They had a fairly silent and perfunctory meal together. After a short review of the day and checklist plan for Tuesday, Jack and Atlanta crawled wearily into their sleeping capsules and both quickly crashed out.

After breakfast on day two, Tuesday 16 February, Atlanta drove the Rover about a kilometre south of the camp. This took them close to the crater they had visited on the test run back in early January. Once again in the distance through the mountains they marvelled at the magnificent spectacle of Olympus Mons, towering majestically above everything else on the reddish skyline. Day two's plan was to take test drillings and rock samples, mainly for comparison with the original samples taken in January. Jack allowed Atlanta to conduct low-intensity drills so that they both increased their operational field experience. The deep-drilling for iron ore and other mineral samples would not be effected until they reached the target site near Uranius Patera, as close to Olympus Mons as the project would take them.

The drilling and sampling took about three hours and they were back at the pod by early afternoon. After lunch, they checked the Rover's computing, functioning, mechanics, and batteries. They discovered two of the twelve lithium batteries were depleted. Better news than expected, although, it was a two-man job to replace the two heavy batteries. Effectively their day's work was completed by about three in the afternoon. After Atlanta had radioed back the daily report with control, Jack made an early dinner for them. After dinner, they sat in the cramped glass pod and marvelled at the beautiful reddish-purple and pink-hued Martian sunset.

After dark they sat silently in awe, watching the Milky Way making its imperceptible rotation in the Martian night above their heads. They had a fairly basic telescope with them. Jack and Atlanta tried and failed to spot the gas cloud, the remnant of the destroyed Earth and Moon, before calling it a night.

Days three and four were similar in scope and plan to the previous two days. They continued further west across the fringes of Western Arabia Terra, with a two night stop at Base Camp II. The weather remained sunny and calm. The test drilling and sampling presented them without any issues.

*

Now Thursday, the end of day four, and Atlanta brought the Rover to a stop as close as possible to the tiny airlock for Base Camp III. She smiled wistfully at Jack.

"I don't know about you, but I'm famished. I could eat a scabby horse!"

Jack, reawakened from his dozy state, spoke softly, not quite sure where his words emanated from.

"Well, I don't know about you, but I'm hungry for something else. I could kiss a beautiful girl."

All Atlanta said was, *well, get on with it then.*

Chapter 28

That same evening, Cortopassi had called the Protetto-rato together for a top-secret meeting. He knew he was taking major risks in attending. As newly elected Pope on Mars, it was difficult for him to leave the New Vatican surreptitiously, without some prying eyes upon him. However, he had brought along a new face that night. It would give him a good cover story for being out without protection from the Swiss Guard security corps.

After moderating the meeting with prayer, and they had performed the blooding ritual, Cortopassi called it to order.

"Brothers of the Protettorato, I apologise for calling another emergency meeting so soon. I realise we generally only meet once a year, as a rule, to maintain a low profile. However, as you know the UCB Rover project is now making its way towards the Cydonian Plain."

He paused for effect and the assembly nodded solemnly.

"Of course, Sinclair and his assistant aren't out there searching for the Seal of the Revelation. But, my fear is they could stumble across it, even by accident. I – rather we – can't allow this to happen."

Another round of nodding heads. Cortopassi turned to look at the new face he had brought to the meeting.

"Brothers, you all know Cardinal Malvoli. What you don't know is, he recently assisted me in getting elected during the voting process, allowing me to become the Holy Father. It is my greatest honour and I'd like to thank the Cardinal for his help."

Malvoli bowed to Cortopassi, somewhat sycophantical-ly.

"My pleasure to help you beat Cardinal MacEachen, Grand Master. I'm here tonight to assist in any way I can."

"Much appreciated. So to that end, the first order of business on the agenda is to elect Cardinal Malvoli as a member of the Protettorato. Can I have a proposer and seconder?"

Blackfriar Balcanguel proposed. Father Tomek Turkowski seconded. Cortopassi lowered his voice, almost to a whisper.

"Now to the main part of the agenda. How to deal with this damned Rover project. Any suggestions, Brothers?"

There was a pregnant pause and then Turkowski spoke up first.

"In your elevated position as Holy Father, you could appeal again to the President. Have him recall the project."

Cortopassi snarled.

"D'you think I haven't thought of that, Tomek? Gold's mesmerised by the thought of Sinclair finding big mineral deposits out there in Cydonia. It would guarantee Gold success in his re-election year. His refusal to listen to me may *just* have cost him the Catholic vote. I'll make sure of that!"

A deathly hush fell in the lowly lit room before Cortopassi continued.

"Any other suggestions?"

The scowling Balcanguel pushed both hands firmly down on the table, slowly rising to his feet.

"Elimination!"

Cortopassi pretended he was aghast, however, he was just conducting the orchestra to play his score.

"Elimination, Friar? What d'you mean?"

"Sinclair and Caie need to be eliminated before they reach Cydonia. We need to kill them."

Cortopassi noted some fearful faces around the table. Turkowski was genuinely aghast.

"Grand Master, is this the only solution? In God's name, we have already had one person killed. Jaap, the university security guard. Are we going to end up with a trail of blood across Mars, so that we can keep our great secret protected?"

Cortopassi's face reddened, but before he could answer, the still-standing Balcanguel pumped the table with his fist as he exploded.

"Yes, we bloody well are! Earth's destruction was God's judgment on mankind and, to avoid us suffering the same fate, it is necessary to punish those threatening the sanctity of the Protettorato."

Turkowski visibly shrunk in his seat, thinking, *this guy is a complete psycho*. Cortopassi raised his arms with outward spreading palms in a placatory motion.

"Brothers, brothers. Let's calm down. I'm sure we all thought this order a bit of an old boys' club and the actions taken back on Earth had ensured the secrecy of the Seal. We wouldn't need to do much to assure its eternal protection. Well, brothers, you're wrong. And Balcanguel – if a little hot-headed tonight – is correct. We must do anything and everything to act as the Protettorato. If that means the project has to be eliminated – then that's what we intend to do!"

A smirking Balcanguel, who had remained upright, spoke triumphantly.

"Grand Master, I applaud your wisdom. I'd sincerely offer my services to carry out the necessary deed. However, that Rover's well beyond even my reach. How do we eliminate them before they can reach the Cydonian Plain?"

Balcanguel sat down. Cortopassi said nothing. He waved an introductory palm towards Malvoli, who spoke slowly and measuredly to the assembly.

"I've got an insider in the Swiss Guard. The guy is a bit of a nut job. But he's one hundred percent loyal to me. If I gave him an order, he'd carry it out without question. He's in charge of the Guards' ordnance depot, which, believe it or not, is quite an arsenal. He's access to two fully-armed military drones. All I have to do is give him the word and he will deploy them against any perceived threat to the Protettorato."

There were a few gasps including Turkowski. Balcanguel's eyes rolled back in ecstasy.

"Excellent, Cardinal Malvoli, excellent!"

"Thank you, Friar. However, there is only one drawback. The drones were designed to protect the confines of the New Vatican and the Holy Father within the city. Their range and scope are limited. If the UCB Rover makes it to Base Camp IV, then the drones can't make it that far and carry out an attack. We know from the CBTV news they're currently at Base Camp III. In other words, we must deploy immediately."

Cortopassi answered affirmatively.

"Deploy!"

Cortopassi then closed the meeting with prayer.

Chapter 29

Jack awoke on Friday morning, day five. He looked wistfully at the still sleeping Atlanta. He wondered how they had managed to make love in the tiny, cramped camp-pod last night. It had involved a lot of laughter and giggling. But, it had been wonderful. Atlanta slowly came to, turning in her capsule, lazily stretching her arms.

"Hello, lover."

Jack blushed pink.

"Hello, you too. I love you, Atlanta."

"I love you too, Jack. But we've got a heckuva journey ahead today. So we better keep things on a professional level."

Jack concurred and they both arose. After breakfast, they made their preparations for the next stage in the project. The plan was to drive the Rover over the last of the rough crater-pocked terrain of the Western Arabia Terra to Base Camp IV. The camp sat on the edge of Cydonia Mensae, the eastern region of the Cydonian Plain, known to be a sandy desert region with flat-topped mesa-like features. It would take them the best part of a day's drive to reach the next camp before sunset, so they wasted no time in setting off. They would share the drive, Jack taking the first shift.

After about an hour's drive from Base Camp III, across very slow, difficult, rocky terrain, a crackle came over the radio. The shift controller back at Cee-Bee spoke.

"Control to UCB Rover X. Can you read me? Over."

Jack kept driving on and nodded to Atlanta to take the call.

"UCB Rover X. Reading you loud and clear. Over."

The controller crackled back on the airwaves.

"Atlanta, we have just received a weather report from Cee-Bee Weather Center. Over."

Atlanta joked back.

"Don't tell me. We can expect rain later. Over."

It never rained on Mars, although it did snow at the poles.

"Yeah, very funny, Atlanta. No this is serious. The day's forecast is for an increasing incidence of dust devils, with a high probability of a full-blown Martian dust storm later today or tonight. Over."

Atlanta gave Jack a worried look and he reciprocated. The infamous dust storms could arise at any time of year, however, the project planning forecast had determined they were low-risk this month.

"What d'you reckon, Jack? Should we head back to Camp III and hunker down for another day?"

Jack pondered on Atlanta's questions.

"My view is we press on to four. See if we can beat the weather. The timescales and camp resources are too tight for us to lose a day's schedule. If we beat the storm, we can hunker down at Cydonia Mensae camp for a day or more if required. If the storm persists, we might need to skip test drilling tomorrow."

"Okay, Jack, you're the boss. I'll radio it in."

Chapter 30

Balcanguel had been tasked by Cortopassi to command the strike against the Rover. Using a Swiss Guard all-terrain armoured carrier driven by Guardsman Hans Graetzer, they had left through the western air-lock. The same one used by Jack and Atlanta on the previous Monday. The military half-track vehicle, similar in design to those used by ice miners at the Martian poles, except fitted with mounted submachine guns. It also carried the two armed drones, with heat-seeking missiles. The ones Malvoli had offered at the secret Protettorato meeting the previous evening.

Graetzer drove the half-track over the hilly terrain, about three miles from the city pods. Well away from prying eyes. As the Swiss Guard parked on the far side of a large crater, he noticed the wind picking up, gently rocking the vehicle.

"Hmm, the dust devils are getting persistent. Not the best day for flying drones."

Balcanguel growled back at Graetzer.

"Just make sure you don't fly those drones into a dust devil and screw up this mission!"

"Well, I'll do my best. But it's difficult enough flying these two babies in formation on a good day. Never mind trying to factor in wind and devils."

Balcanguel became increasingly impatient with the Swiss Guard.

"Look, Graetzer, let's just get moving. We don't have a lot of time to play with. How long d'you reckon it'll take to fly to the strike zone?"

Graetzer did the math before answering the black-cloaked cleric, who he was beginning to resent. However, Cardinal Malvoli had ordered him to follow Balcanguel's instructions to the letter. He was loyal in the extreme to Malvoli and would not disobey his master. Graetzer decided to concentrate on getting this mission over and done with.

"It should be about four hours' flying time and we only get one shot at this. The drones won't have enough fuel to get them back to Cee-Bee. After we make the kill, we just have to land them somewhere out on the Arabia Terra. Might be able to recover them down the line, but they'll probably just be write-offs."

"We'll worry about that later, Graetzer. Meantime, let's get them in the air and get this thing finished."

Chapter 31

Jack was worried. They had been driving for a good few hours now. Battling into the strong westerly wind. Trying to dodge the larger of the dust devils slowing the Rover down. It was becoming increasingly likely they would not make Base Camp IV before nightfall. Although the Rover had powerful arc lighting, it was not an ideal situation to be travelling in the rugged Martian terrain in the dark. The lights would use up a lot of battery power, a scarce resource they could not afford to squander.

They discussed the possibility of 'hunkering down' for the night. This entailed using an inbuilt design-feature of the Rover, which deployed an encapsulation system, covering the exposed working mechanics and wheels. In an emergency, the Rover could park out in the Martian wilderness overnight, away from a campsite if necessary. The Rover was stocked with emergency rations for Jack and Atlanta to fall back on. They agreed to 'hunker down' if they were forced into it, rather than driving on in the dark. They did not want to end up crashing down some unseen ravine.

Chapter 32

Ewan Sinclair had been here once before, many years ago, under a previous incumbent of the Oval Office. That had been to receive his promotion to Emeritus Professor. He was bemused as to why Elijah Gold had asked him to a meeting this morning. Ewan had been at home watching Jill's breakfast news report, looking for some progress on Jack's project. Jill reported only minor details. The Rover was still on schedule, although they were keeping an eye on adverse weather developments.

"Professor Sinclair, before we get started, let me introduce my Chief of Police Kurt Reich. Don't know if you two guys have met?"

They both shook their heads in the negative. It occurred to Ewan that Reich would probably be heading up the investigation into Joe Jaap's shooting at UCB.

Jeez, Ewan thought, *have they found something that puts me back in the frame for murder.*

Ewan and Reich shook hands and the President began the meeting.

"Professor Sinclair, Kurt here's been deeply involved in the crime that took place on campus. The one you were the only witness to. First up, let me state, we think you're completely in the clear. I'll let Kurt take up the story."

Ewan gave an audible blow of relief. The Chief of Police reported his findings.

"Yes, Professor Sinclair, our investigations have revealed evidence that points to a hooded man making his way from an east-side locus of the city towards the university campus. I know my officers have asked you this before. But think back. Did you get a look at the hooded man's face? Was it someone you recognised?"

Ewan shook his head slowly.

"I'm sorry. He kept his head down and the hood up. I've

no idea who he was."

"Okay, Professor. However, we've been able to identify the likely suspect. We also think he may have been in cahoots with other actors."

Ewan was taken aback.

"Joe Jaap was killed by some group. Who was the hooded man and who were the others?"

Gold interjected.

"Professor, at present, we're not at liberty to state names. We still haven't joined all the dots on this one. But we believe there is some sort of high-ranking conspiracy going on here. Carry on, Kurt."

"Our conclusions regarding the contract killing of the security guard is he was taken out, on the basis, he either knew something or had seen something, probably on campus. Ewan, it's still all very tenuous and inconclusive. We think maybe, just maybe, there's some link between you and your son."

Ewan was incredulous.

"What are you saying? Joe Jaap was killed regarding something to do with me and Jack? Mr. President, what the hell does this all mean?"

Gold spoke softly, but firmly.

"Ewan, may I call you Ewan? What Kurt suspects is there is something that links you to your son Jack, particularly to his current on-going UCB Rover X project. Is there anything you can think of along those lines?"

Ewan stroked his chin thoughtfully and shook his head slowly.

"Not really, Mr. President. I'm an astrophysicist and Jack is a geologist, so I've not been directly involved in his project. I know he's seen you a couple of times, discussing budget authority and such. I can't see where Joe Jaap would fit into that."

Kurt Reich took the reins again.

"Professor, I'll ask you a question. Think as deeply as you can on an answer. As I say, we've several suspects, who we think may be co-conspirators. Possibly, you may have run into one or more of them. Thinking back to the days before Jaap's murder, was there anyone who may have aroused your suspicions on any matter at all? Not necessarily directly related to the killing?"

Ewan was flustered.

"I'm really not sure what you're getting at, Kurt."

"Okay, Ewan, I'm going to try and be a bit more specific. I'll try and jog your memory. If I said to you, was there anyone in the clergy who may have caught you unawares or aroused your suspicion, does that mean anything to you?"

"The clergy? What like a minister or a – p – priest?"

"Has something just struck you?"

Ewan thought back. His memory played tricks with him, due to the head injury. Was it before Joe Jaap's murder, or was it after. No, it was definitely a good few days before in his office at UCB. Definitely before!

"Professor?"

"The rocks. Is it something to do with the rocks?"

Both Gold and Reich looked completely bemused.

"What rocks?"

"Father Tomek Turkowski saw the photos of the rocks. Was he the one who hacked into my computer?"

Gold thumped the presidential seal on his desk.

"Bingo! That's the link, Kurt. Now, Ewan, you better tell us all about these rocks."

Chapter 33

The juddering drive to Camp IV had become onerous and treacherous due to the worsening storm. Atlanta had taken a short stint on the drive, for about an hour or so. However, her arms had started to ache badly. Jack had taken over for the last few hours. Even he began to feel the stresses and strains in his arms and shoulders. Trying to avoid the increased number of dust devils became nigh on impossible. The Rover was tossed about like an old wooden barque on a stormy sea. Jack turned to Atlanta and saw the worry etched across her face. He was also concerned that if a particularly large and violent dust devil caught the Rover amidships, it could upend the vehicle.

Then the whole project would be in real trouble and they would be in peril for their lives. Jack half-shouted to Atlanta above the roar of the gathering storm.

"I think we better hunker down and deploy the encapsulation system. What d'you think?"

Atlanta surveyed the swirling dust massing all around them. Then something else caught her eye. About three kilometres ahead she spotted the edge of the desert of the Cydonia Mensae, but it also looked a dark blur at first glance.

She pointed ahead.

"My God, Jack. Look!"

Jack squinted his eyes and strained to see through the devils pounding them left and right. He saw what Atlanta was staring at. A huge wall of red dust, at least fifty metres high, pummelling its way straight towards them.

"We need to deploy encapsulation!"

Before they could think about carrying out that procedure, they were both startled by another distraction, coming from their rear.

*

Back in the half-track, Graetzer had been struggling manfully to manoeuvre the two drones in synch, keeping them as high as he could, to avoid the worst of the swirling columns of dust. Each drone carried two heat-seeking missiles, giving him four shots at the target. Suddenly, he turned to Balcanguel and shouted.

"There it is. Target. Two and a half kilometres dead ahead."

Balcanguel examined the monitor. It had a webcam feed coming back from the lead drone's camera. He could just make out the Rover. The vehicle appeared to be struggling in the storm.

"When can you make the shot?"

"Anytime within two kilometres from target."

"Okay, make the kill!"

A few minutes later, Graetzer checked the distance on the scope and fixed his sightline on the target. *Two kilometres*, he thought to himself. He had a clear line of sight to the Rover. A good time to shoot. He pressed the button and a heat-seeker fired away from the lead drone. It was looking like a good kill.

Balcanguel and Graetzer watched silently as the deadly missile pursued the unsuspecting target. Then, out of nowhere, a gigantic dust devil swept across the monitor. The top of the swirling column almost miraculously arced itself gracefully into the path of the missile. There was enough thermal energy generated within the dust devil to attract the attention of the heat-seeker. It sought out this new target. It exploded violently into the dust column. It dissipated the energy within the whirling devil, causing it to collapse on itself.

*

This was the problem to the rear that had distracted Jack and Atlanta from the onrushing wall of the Martian dust storm.

"Jesus, Jack, what was that? Lightning?"

Jack had looked back through the rear windscreen, a split second after the explosion, seeing the ball of fire emanating from the collapsing dust column. He came to a quick conclusion.

"That's no lightning strike, Atlanta. Something or someone is attacking us. We need to take evasive action. We need to head straight for that wall of dust. Now!"

*

Back in the half-track Balcanguel exploded with rage, slamming his hand across the back of Graetzer's head, as he peered at the monitor.

"You damned idiot, you've missed them. We've lost the element of surprise. Look at them, they're zigzagging to try and take avoiding action. They're heading straight for the dust storm. If they get in there, we'll lose them."

Graetzer examined the computer readouts on his monitor. Firing the missile had seriously reduced the power cells on the lead drone. It was on its last legs.

"I need to land the lead drone now, or it's going to crash and burn."

Balcanguel snarled.

"We've no time for that. If we lose it, we lose it. Just fire the goddam second missile."

Graetzer stared again at the monitor. The Rover was about half a kilometre away from the wall of dust. Once in there, he would have no target to bear on. Graetzer struggled to get a good sight on the crazily zigzagging Rover, now almost enveloped in dust devils. Maintaining a steady flight path for the faltering drone in the howling windstorm became almost impossible. He closed his eyes, fired the button, hoping for the best, as the missile shot towards the target. Meantime, he saw from the webcam the drone nosediving towards the Martian surface.

*

Atlanta screamed at the sudden noise. She looked back through the rear windscreen and saw an explosion on the ground behind them, not realising it was the crashing drone.

Then she saw the trail from the missile.

"Jack! There's a missile coming straight for us. Do something!"

He thought as quickly as possible. The Rover still had about two hundred metres to reach the oncoming dust storm. *Too far*, he thought. He had seen that the last missile had been distracted by a dust devil and he saw a large one ahead. He knew it was risky, but he had to aim for it.

"Hold on tight, Atlanta! I'm going to drive into that devil. We'll be tossed about like a toy car."

The Rover slammed into the bottom of the swirling column. Jack and Atlanta felt the vehicle slowly rise from the Martian surface. It began to rotate violently.

The second heat-seeker became tricked, just like the first missile. It turned its attention to the rising column of hot red dust. Jack and Atlanta felt the explosion above them and saw the ball of flames spreading out through the atmosphere. Again, the explosion took all the energy out of the dust devil. It quickly collapsed, dropping the Rover down about three metres with a crumping thud.

Jack quickly realised they had been lucky on two counts. They had now crossed into the sandy desert of the Cydonia Mensae and they had a fairly soft landing. By some miracle, they had also landed facing the onrushing storm. He immediately gunned down on the accelerator. The Rover's wheels bit purposefully into the sandy soil and surged forward.

*

Balcanguel screamed at Graetzer to fire the remaining two missiles. The Swiss Guard instinctively knew it was too late. He could do nothing to stop the second drone ploughing into the wall of red dust. The screen went all fuzzy, then blacked out. He knew the drone had exploded in mid-air, without discharging its missiles. Graetzer turned to face the Blackfriar, incandescent with rage.

Balcanguel drew out a stiletto from his black cloak and threatened Graetzer with it.

"You incompetent bastard, Graetzer. You have failed your mission. I'm going to make you pay for that failure."

Before Balcanguel could make a move towards him, Graetzer pointed back in the direction of Cee-Bee. Balcanguel looked back through the rear bullet-proof glass window of the half-track. He spotted two air-cars from the Cee-Bee Police Department descending speedily towards them with flashing lights and sirens blaring.

Graetzer spoke calmly, with a tinge of sarcasm.

"Looks like we both failed."

Chapter 34

Ewan and Jill sat hugging each other in the Control Room, frantic with worry. On Saturday morning, day six, the Rover had not arrived at Base Camp IV as scheduled. The dust storm still raged across Cydonia Mensae. Radio contact with Jack and Atlanta had been cut off by the lightning storm raging above the dust clouds.

The shift controller kept firing out a periodic message.

"UCB Rover X. This is Cee-Bee control. Do you read me? Over."

All he got back was the heavy crackle of static.

Chapter 35

Kurt Reich's Police Department had a busy night, Friday into Saturday. After they had arrested Balcanguel and Graetzer outside the city, an arrest warrant was issued for Father Tomek Turkowski. Under interrogation, Turkowski agreed to provide information on the secret organisation of the Protettorato and its members.

"I assure you, Chief Reich, I never agreed to the increasing levels of violence."

In return for his testimony, he pleaded for leniency in sentencing. Reich could not believe the names Turkowski surrendered up; including among many others, David Balcanguel, Robertus Algeo, Cardinals Malvoli, and John O'Carroll. And, unbelievably, the Pope elect, Benedetto Cortopassi. He issued arrest warrants for all of the known Protettorato, except Cortopassi. The Chief of Police issued an order to place Cortopassi under strict house arrest until he could speak to President Gold in the morning, to discuss the delicate situation.

It was not going to look good having an incoming Holy Father involved in criminal and nefarious activities.

Turkowski admitted repentantly to Reich.

"I was aware Balcanguel had been ordered to kill Joe Jaap because the guard had seen me outside Professor Sinclair's office at UCB. Jaap's killing was needless. I'm certain the security guard had no genuine suspicions as to what I'd been up to."

Turkowski also stated it took very little to incite the sadistic Blackfriar into mindless violence. He also confessed to hacking into Professor Sinclair's computer and stealing files, including the photos of the rocks.

"However, under pain of death, Chief, there's nothing that'll make me confess to the purpose of the Protettorato, or what it's sworn to protect."

Reich found the same wall of silence from all the other arrested members of the secret sect. None of them would admit to why they had conspired to disrupt and disable the UCB Rover X project.

Chapter 36

Later on Saturday morning, Elijah Gold and Kurt Reich took an air-limo to Cortopassi's residence. It was surrounded by armed cops, keeping him under house arrest. Cortopassi had been told nothing, although, he must have guessed much of what had been transpiring throughout the night. When they were ushered into his main office, the Pope elect raged and railed against the President and Chief of Police.

"This is an outrage, Mr. President! Keeping me a prisoner in my own home. And you an old friend of mine too. You and Reich better have a good explanation for this unwarranted slur on the office of the papacy."

Gold raised a placatory palm towards Cortopassi.

"Benny, all in good time. The Chief of Police will explain everything we know so far about the goings-on of your secret little club. The Protettorato. As for being old friends, I'm not so sure. I guess we just used each other for political expediency. Okay, Kurt, over to you."

Reich opened his file and laid all the evidence they had gathered over weeks on the Protettorato and its Grand Master. Cortopassi listened unblinkingly and impassively. Reich detailed the surveillance on Balcanguel, trailing back from the scene of Joe Jaap's shooting to the meeting with Cortopassi in his air-limo. Balcanguel had also confessed to the killing as ordered by the Grand Master. Reich also detailed Turkowski's confession to break into Professor Sinclair's UCB computer and being disturbed by Joe Jaap, which sealed his unfortunate fate. This linked the files and the photos of the rocks between the Professor's investigations and the Protettorato's desire to terminate his son Jack's geological project.

Algeo and the others all confessed they had been at secret meetings to agree on a plan to have the project stopped at any cost. Cardinal Malvoli confessed to knowing the late Holy Father had been murdered by the radical Wim Wendtlander in collusion with Cortopassi. Malvoli had also agreed to manipulate the voting in the New Vatican to ensure Cortopassi was elected Pope. He was promised the promotion as the new Camerlengo.

Malvoli also confessed to recruiting the Swiss Guard Hans Graetzer to act in collusion with Balcanguel to destroy the Rover, using unauthorised Vatican armoured hardware.

Cortopassi corrected Reich.

"As Pope elect, I gave Cardinal Malvoli full authority to deploy those drones."

Gold was stunned and Reich scribbled a note.

"You realise you have just made an incriminatory remark?"

Cortopassi shrugged.

"But, Benny, why? What the hell is all this about? What's out there Jack Sinclair mustn't discover?"

It dawned on Cortopassi, even with all the detailed confessions that Reich presented, the members of the Protettorato had kept to their bond of blood.

"Ah, Eli, that's one thing we will all take to the grave. So, Chief Reich, are you going to arrest me now?"

Reich looked to the President, who shook his head.

"Benny, how d'you think it would look if the head of the Roman Catholic Church on Mars was found to be involved in secret societies, murder, and conspiracy to murder? Jeez, it could signal the end of the church. No, I don't think that would be a good idea. Same as I don't think having you inaugurated as Pope would be a responsible thing either. I'm sure Cardinal MacEachen will make a fine replacement."

"And me, Mr. President? What are you going to do with me?"

"Benny, you've been under a great strain recently. You took the killing of the late Pope badly. The stress of being thrust into the papal limelight has become too much for you. In a few days, Cardinal MacEachen and I will announce you have suffered a complete nervous breakdown. You will retire to the Eastern Sanatorium on health grounds."

"The Eastern Sanatorium? Eli. That is a secure mental institution."

Gold nodded.

"And we'll make sure you're kept secure there for the rest of your life."

Chapter 37

Hours had passed by. Ewan, Jill, and the shift controller were all half-dozing in their uncomfortable chairs when a crackle came over the airwaves. Faint and breaking up, but it was Jack.

"UCB – Rover – X – to – Control. *[Shssssh]* – Read – over?"

The three of them were simultaneously startled into action. The controller grabbed his mic.

"Hi, Jack! Reading you loud and clear. What's your SitRep? Over."

Jack battled through electrical interference to update the controller.

"We're both alive, unharmed, physically, and mentally well. We came under some sort of unexpected attack and raced to hide in the dust storm. The moment we'd been swallowed up in the dust, we deployed the encapsulation. It worked perfectly to protect us. We've spent the night hunkered down in the Cydonian desert. The main storm had now passed through and it's now confined to strong winds and frequent dust devils. Over."

The de-encapsulation process had been a bigger issue, mainly due to the build-up of the fine red sand around the vehicle. The Rover half-entombed had to be de-encapsulated in small stages. Jack and Atlanta had to don their surface suits and go out onto the Martian surface to dig the sand away from the Rover. This was tiring and time-consuming work, using up most of the day.

Atlanta reported back on the Rover's systems and schematics. The vehicle monitors reported no material damage to the mechanical or computerised hardware. Just some minor bumps and scrapes. The main worry was the depletion of lithium cells. They were down to sixty percent capacity.

Although the storm had passed, Jack indicated they only had about two hours of usable daylight remaining. They intended to use that time to drive on towards Base Camp IV. This would allow the reactivated solar panels to recharge the lithium batteries to some extent. Jack had one major concern about re-starting the project.

"Control. I'm worried that we will – will be under attack again. God knows what that was all about. Over."

The controller indicated to Ewan to respond. He bent over to the mic.

"Hi, son. It's your dad here. Um, eh, over."

"Dad! Oh, God, Dad. It's – it's...."

Ewan heard his son's voice break with raw emotion and he responded with a huge lump in his throat.

"Mum's here too, Jack. Thank God you and Atlanta are still – still alive. Look, Jack. That thing about the attack. It's all being taken care of at this end and you're now both safe. You wouldn't believe what's been going on. Even the President had to intervene. Eh, over."

"Copy that. But, Dad, I don't understand. Why's some-one trying to destroy us with missiles? Over."

Ewan explained it all had something to do with the Gary Mackintosh files and the cryptic messages on the rock photos that he, Jack, and Jai had examined. As none of the culprits arrested were disclosing the secret of the rocks, all Ewan could suggest was for Jack and Atlanta to look out for clues as they progressed into Cydonia.

"Okay, will do, Dad. We need to get going or we'll lose the light. Say hi to Mum and *we* love you both. Over."

Ewan handed the mic back to the controller. He and Jill hugged each other with relief. Jill felt a flutter of new life in her womb. She prayed things were taking a turn for the better. She giggled to her husband.

"Well, Ewan Sinclair. *We* love you both. Now that sounds interesting, doesn't it?"

Ewan laughed heartily, releasing the pent up emotion of the last few hours.

Chapter 38

It took another eight less eventful days for Jack and Atlanta to drive the Rover to their final destination at Base Camp VIII. They were a day behind schedule, due to being held up by the violent storm and the unexpected attack. However, they could recover time on the return trip. They only stopped for one night at Base Camp IV, mainly to change the depleted lithium cells. No rock sampling or test borings were carried out to make up for the lost time.

Base Camp V involved another two-night stay, located in the centre of the Cydonia Mensae. They had driven out to examine the mesa-like flat-topped hills that were prevalent in this region. They took rock samples and extracted some test bores. Their initial view was these flat-topped hills were constituted of similar mesa-forming stratified rock, also found in the Western Arabia Terra. They would be examined in greater depth back in the lab.

They also visited the Martian mythological geological anomaly known as *The Face on Mars*. This was an almost regular pyramid-shaped hill feature, which in low-res photographs from early Mars missions, displayed the psychological phenomenon of pareidolia. From above, the optical illusion made it look like a human face. Jack and Atlanta were less than impressed with this geological outcrop. It seemed to be another fairly bulk standard mesa, which had been shaped and pointed by the Martian wind and weather over millennia.

They steered a more north-westerly course skirting through the hillier Cydonia Colles region and crossed intersecting valleys of the Cydonia Labyrinthus region to the southern edge of the great plains of the Acidilia Planitius. The vast Acidilia Planitius desert stretched for two thousand miles to the Martian North Pole.

Another two nights were spent at Base Camp VI.

On the survey day, they drove the Rover about fifteen kilometres north to the edge of the huge Arandas Crater. They found a well-worn and heavily-littered track that took them up and over into the crater. The Arandas Crater was one of the outer limits for the fabled Martian ice miners, who camped in shift rotations during the Martian winter months, mining the huge ice water and dry ice deposits. They could see the currently deserted ramshackle buildings about three kilometres away. Jack surveyed the camp through his telescope.

"Let's not bother going over there. We'll just do our test borings here at the inner edge of the crater."

Extensive soil samples were scooped from the floor of the Acidilia Planitius to review back at the lab. The opinion was this flat, dust-filled plain was once a huge ocean. If correct, it may have supported life forms millions of years ago.

Taking a more south-westerly course from the Arandas Crater, the next two nights were spent at Base Camp VII in the Chryse Planitia region. This was a pre-planned rest and recuperation stage, before reaching their ultimate goal. Jack and Atlanta used this rest stop at Camp VII to get to know each other intimately.

"Atlanta, I love you."

"I love you too, Jack."

It took a further day's driving for the Rover to reach Base Camp VIII. This involved climbing into the foothills of the vast Tempe Terra mountain range and arriving at their camp pod in the Kasei Valles. They could see the mound of the volcanic Uranius Patera, twenty kilometres to the west. It would be their geological survey site the following day. Beyond that, they marvelled at the awesome sight of Olympus Mons towering up into the Martian atmosphere. Had Gold not curtailed the budget the plan had been to do some exploratory geological surveying at the largest volcano in the solar system. That would have to wait for a future project. However, Jack and Atlanta were excited about the following day's survey at Uranius Patera.

Chapter 39

After a hearty breakfast, they set off with huge anticipation for the base of the Uranius Patera volcano. Here Jack's initial surveys, using long-range geo-mapping satellites, suggested the distinct possibility of iron ore and other mineral deposits.

If he and Atlanta could find the mother lode, then the project investment from Gold's Congressional budget would be repaid in spades.

It was an arduous and gruelling climb for the Rover after the relative flatness of the Cydonian desert. They had to keep stopping to check their detailed GPS navigator. This was to ensure they did not go off course, find themselves facing some deep chasm, or get trapped in a tight gully. The journey to the dormant volcano took an hour longer than planned.

When they reached the research site, they sat in awe of the great flat-topped volcano. Dry ice gas tumbled out of the summit of the Patera, resembling fountain-like clouds pouring down the conical sides of the volcano. The omnipresent Olympus Mons, thirty kilometres away, provided an even more impressive backdrop to Uranius Patera.

"Wow, Atlanta! Have you ever seen anything like this?"

"No, Jack, it's magnificent. Although, I guess we're not here for the view."

Jack quickly agreed. They donned their surface suits, for the morning's work ahead, planning to do a recce of the volcano's base to identify the best test sites for rock sampling and test boring. Due to the extremely cold Martian atmosphere, which the thermostat indicated currently -48ºC, their heavily padded surface suits were good for up to an hour and a half outside the Rover.

They edged gingerly across the rubble-strewn volcanic foothills, the padded surface suits their only protection from the toxic Martian atmosphere.

As the pale Martian sun approached its zenith, Jack pointed out a rubble field about a hundred metres ahead. Walking towards it, the sun made the field of rocks sparkle and glint with reflected light. They both started lifting and inspecting the chunks of golden-hued crystallised minerals. Jack radioed to Atlanta on his headset.

"Jeez, Atlanta. This is a promising start. Iron pyrites, Fool's Gold, loads of the stuff, just scattered here all over the surface. Bound to be a vein underground."

Some small deposits of iron pyrites had been found in the Western Arabia Terra near Cee-Bee. Pyrites was used in various manufacturing processes and a key component in the vital lithium batteries used widely in the city. Even surveying the surface deposits of the shiny Fool's Gold at Uranius Patera was enough to get Jack and Atlanta excited.

"God, Jack. We've only been here half an hour and already we've found payback on the project."

Jack quipped.

"Yep, we can repay Gold with Fool's Gold!"

Jack took some readings with his portable magnetometer and Atlanta did the same with her small Geiger counter. Atlanta spoke first.

"The Geiger isn't showing much above ambient Martian radiation levels. There is very little radioactive material in the ground here. A bit disappointing."

Jack was more effusive.

"The magnetometer is off the scale here. Suggests there could be significant deposits of magnetised iron ore in this region. All we need to do is discover where to start boring. We've got fifteen minutes left. The meter indicates we keep walking in a westerly direction."

They continued west across the rubble and sparkling pyrites-strewn volcanic rock-field. They soon spotted an outcrop of large conjoined hexagonal black basalt-like columns and recorded them for later sampling with the Rover's equipment.

Basalt rock, once molten lava spewed out by Uranius Patera, was also very iron-rich. Another indicator they were in the right region for iron ore fields. They straddled carefully around the outcrop of basalt. The Martian sun had reached its midday apex. A flash of bright light startled and dazzled both of them.

Chapter 40

Their helmet visors quickly readjusted to the flashing light. It was caused by the sun reflecting off objects, about three hundred metres downslope from their position at the basalt outcrop. Jack shouted through his headset.

"Atlanta! What the hell do they look like to you?"

Atlanta squinted her eyes to focus on the dazzling objects.

"My God, Jack. They look like the tops of three pyramids. Pyramids made of Fool's Gold. How the hell...?"

Jack tapped his wrist symbolically to indicate their time had elapsed. They needed to make their way back to the Rover. After recording the coordinates of the pyramidal pyrites, they headed back. They could feel the chill starting to creep into their surface suits.

Chapter 41

Back in the Rover, they excitedly discussed this morning's discoveries over a lunch of soya burgers and baked beans. Jack was effusive as he read over their findings.

"What a start, Atlanta. Iron pyrites, basalt-like rock, pyrites pyramids. And we've only been researching for an hour and a half."

"It's astounding, Jack. What d'you make of those pyramids? They look man-made, but we're the first humans to venture this far west in any meaningful sense of the word."

Jack was thoughtful.

"I know, although, they may just be naturally formed. Back on Earth, pyrites could form into large cuboid crystals. Of course, nothing in the scale of these pyramidal shaped ones. Maybe Martian geology has allowed for bigger and better crystallisation of the pyrites."

"Maybe. Although did you notice one thing about the pyramids?"

He had, however, he let Atlanta blurt it out.

"If you looked back at the midday sun and you drew an imaginary line through the pyramids and continued onto Olympus Mons. Jack, they were all in a straight line!"

Jack nodded in agreement.

"And what's the probability of Mother Nature managing that?"

Outside, a small dust storm had kicked off. They decided to postpone taking the Rover to the research sites until the following day. They spent the rest of the afternoon in Camp VIII pod cataloguing their findings and reporting back to Cee-Bee Control, although they made no mention of the strange pyramids. They wanted to examine them up close and personal before jumping to any conclusions.

Chapter 42

Cortopassi knew this was his last throw of the dice.

This was his last night under house arrest. Tomorrow President Gold and Cardinal MacEachen would jointly announce the Pope elect would be retiring due to health reasons. He would be taken by Chief of Police Reich to the Eastern Sanatorium, where he would spend the rest of his life.

Well, Gold has got another thing coming, if he thinks he's going to lock me up in that hell-hole!

Cortopassi sat in his private study, on the pretence of writing personal letters and sending final emails. Outside were posted two of Gold's Secret Service agents. The locks had been removed on the study doors. He silently took a chair over and jammed it under the door handles.

He moved quickly over to his bookcase and pressed the hidden lever. The bookcase slid back to reveal a secret passageway, which he slipped into, closing the bookcase behind him. He hurried down the passage. It brought him back up into a heavily-tinted pod in the centre of the Cardinal's garden.

It contained all the accoutrements of his position as Grand Master of the Protettorato, including his secret papers and computer files on the Seal of the Revelation. *These will have to be destroyed*, he thought. It also contained a powerful telescope and an encrypting radio set.

Cortopassi sat at the telescope and scanned the Martian night sky. He knew it was due over Cee-Bee about this time. There it was, right on schedule. Mars Galactica 3. Old, creaking and leaking, but it was still a functioning space station, over thirty years after Space Commander Jack Crossan worked his last shift on it.

Selecting the desired frequency on his radio, Cortopassi transmitted a message up into the outer atmosphere of Mars.

"Red Cardinal to MGal 3. Can you read me? Over."

There were a few minutes of radio silence and then the line hissed and crackled. The receiver sounded somewhat bemused.

"Death's-head Moth to Red Cardinal. Receiving you loud and clear. Over."

Cortopassi breathed a sigh of relief. He checked that the receiver on MGal3 was alone and could speak freely. Death's-head Moth confirmed he was alone in his bunk. Death's-head Moth was Father William Balcanguel, brother of Blackfriar David Balcanguel, now in police custody. Father William, the RC chaplain on MGal3, just as fanatical as his brother, and he was a 'sleeper' agent of the Protettorato. Only Cortopassi and his brother David knew of his secret membership.

"Death's-Head Moth, I need to inform you the police have uncovered our organisation. All members on the surface are in custody, except your Grand Master. I'm under house arrest until tomorrow. We need to take urgent action. Over."

Father William was in complete shock at this turn of events. He quickly regained his composure.

"What d'you need Red Cardinal? Over."

Cortopassi, knowing MGal 3 would soon be out of radio range, quickly brought the *other Balcanguel* up to speed with the developments on Mars, which threatened the Seal of the Revelation. The key point he needed to get across was that the UCB Rover X project had to be terminated. He was able to assess the Rover should now have reached Base Camp VIII at Uranius Patera. Father William knew what that meant, but he needed to hear the *ignition code*.

"What are your requirements Red Cardinal? Over."

"Invoke Operation Bright Light ASAP. Over."

"Death's-head Moth to Red Cardinal. Will comply. Over."

Cortopassi signed off.

"BTW. You will be the new Red Cardinal from tomorrow. Over and out."

Father William Balcanguel was astounded. He had not heard a jot from Cortopassi in nearly eight years. Now he had just been promoted to Grand Master of the Protettorato. He puffed up his chest with pride and prepared to fulfil his destiny.

Back in the dark-tinted garden pod, Cortopassi ripped out the radio equipment and smashed up the telescope. He shredded all his secret papers and wiped his computer clean. Copies of all this material belonging to the Protettorato were stored safely in a secret mountain cave in the Western Arabia Terra, known only to Death's-Head Moth. This would be recovered in due course. It was now up to the new Grand Master to ensure the continuation of the Protettorato.

Finally, Cortopassi ensured the air-lock from the passageway into the garden pod was completely sealed. He sat calmly down at his desk in front of his computer, blinking emptily back at him. He allowed himself a wry smile, opened the desk drawer, and drew out a nickel-plated pistol. Without hesitating, he placed it in his mouth and fired upwards. The bullet sped through his brain and up through the glass pod, blowing a hole into the Martian night.

The sudden change in air pressure caused the pod to explode with all its contents scattering wildly out into the atmosphere. The air-lock held, but the explosion reverberated back along the passageway. It blew the bookcase off its slide-rails.

Outside the Cardinal's study, the two Secret Service agents nearly jumped out their skins with fright.

"Jesus H Christ, what the fuck's that?"

They swiftly moved towards the unlocked door, only to find it barred. It took about thirty seconds for the burly agents to smash through the doors and the offending chair. Their guns were raised and ready. Red dust billowed out of the passageway through the gap created by the bookcase hanging off its rails. They could quickly imagine what had occurred at the other end of the passage. The senior agent turned to his colleague.

"Well, you gonna tell Gold we screwed up, or am I?"

Chapter 43

The next morning, an early radio call from Control startled Jack and Atlanta awake. After the Controller had made the introductions, he passed his mic over to Jack's father. Ewan quickly brought them up to speed with the events of the previous evening.

"Jack, Cortopassi committed suicide in his secret garden pod. Right under the noses of the Secret Service. Over."

Deep down Jack was relieved. Although, he was saddened by another person's life needlessly lost in connection with his project. He found it difficult to reconcile the inconceivable deaths of Jaap, Wendtlander, the Pope, and Cortopassi to what appeared to be an innocuous geological survey. Innocent journalists had been needlessly murdered and even his mother had been almost killed.

Maybe, just maybe, Cortopassi's death would bring this whole sorry saga to an end.

"Well, Dad, let's hope that's the last life lost related to the project. With Cortopassi dead and his cronies in prison, surely Atlanta and I can get on with some peaceful rock-hunting. Over."

"We're not so sure about that at this end. I've had a meeting this morning with President Gold and Kurt Reich. The Police Department and Secret Service have been through Cortopassi's room with a fine toothcomb. Although it was pretty much destroyed in the blast, they found the remnants of a high-end encrypting radio set. They think he was probably in touch with some unknown rogue element of the Protettorato. Over."

"So, what are you saying, Dad? Over."

"Son, we reckon you and Atlanta might still be in some kind of danger. Your mum and I think the two of you should postpone the project. Head back to Cee-Bee immediately. Gold and Reich concur with us. Over."

Ewan and Jill sat by the mic and could hear Jack and

Atlanta murmuring in the background, discussing the situation. Jack came back on.

"Atlanta and I say that's negative. We've come all this way. Our preliminary findings have shown we're in an important geological region. Man's future technological progress on Mars is resting on what we discover. Sorry, Mum and Dad, but we're pressing on. Over."

Ewan and Jill tried their utmost strident paternal and maternal pleadings. Ultimately, they knew Jack's work was too important for him to give up at this crucial stage. Jill signed the call off.

"Okay, son, but the two of you be careful out there. Be on your guard. Over and out."

Chapter 44

They ate breakfast, which, following the radio call, neither had much appetite for. They set off in the Rover. Atlanta took the helm and drove west towards the research sites at the base of Uranius Patera. The call from Ewan and Jill had put them on edge. They were unsure of what to expect. They kept scanning the Martian skies for any drones, which might attack them again. However, the sky remained a clear, peaceful pinkish-blue, the rock-strewn surface was calm and windless, and visibility was excellent.

They planned on the previous evening, to head out today to the three pyramids. They would research those, then work their way back, taking samples and borings at the basalt-like columns, then finally at the pyrites rock-field. It only took about fifteen minutes for Atlanta to drive to the structures. They gleamed golden in the morning sun, rainbow rays bouncing off their peaks in every direction.

"Okay, Atlanta, before we start any boring, let's suit up and get a closer look at these three babies."

Once into their surface suits and helmets, they exited the Rover and scrunched across the red sandy soil to the base of the nearest pyrites pyramid. It rose about five metres above the Martian surface. They each walked in the opposite direction around the perfectly square base, surveying and photographing the object as they went. They met each other on the west side facing Olympus Mons, off in the distance. Jack spoke on his headset.

"Well, Atlanta, first impressions?"

"Jack, it's weird. This thing isn't just one huge cuboidal crystalline structure formed by a natural volcanic reaction."

"That's what I concur too."

"Jack, it's been constructed using blocks of perfectly moulded and carved pyrites. This thing's a genuine goddam Fool's Gold pyramid. Any Egyptian Pharaoh would have given his right arm for one of these!"

"Yep, what we have here's a manufactured pyramid. We've not had the technology in the last twenty-eight years for this to be man-made. Christ, Atlanta, we're only just evolving from the ploughshare and getting back to mid-20th century manufacturing capabilities."

"Jack, if we didn't build this. Who did?"

"God only knows."

They decided to use their shovels to dig down on the west face of the pyramid, mainly to gauge if the pyramid continued sloping downwards and whether it was part of a larger structure. Atlanta chose the middle of the west face to dig. Jack worked at the sharp north-west edge of the pyramid. After half an hour's hard digging it was quite obvious this was part of a much larger pyramid, which had been buried by the soft red Martian dust. They also guessed this was a process that had occurred over a long period, millennia, maybe even eons. The whole thing was beginning to spook them.

They continued scooping away the dust and small rocks from the smooth sides of the pyrites. Then Atlanta's shovel clunked metallically off an obstruction.

"Jack, come and help me dig here?"

Jack returned to the centre of the west face. They both worked more archaeologically than their normal geological fashion, periodically photographing as they proceeded. As they dug down a protruding shape appeared on the smooth side of the pyramid. Once fully uncovered, they could see it was also of intricately carved pyrites, perfectly circular, about a metre in diameter, although still full of dust. Jack held Atlanta a small tool.

"Here, brush it off with this."

Atlanta spent a few minutes gently brushing it. Then they both stepped out of the hole they had dug to examine the fruits of their labour. They stared at each other through their tinted helmet visors for what seemed an eternity. Atlanta spoke hoarsely with a huge lump in her throat.

"Jack, what – what's that look like to you?"

Jack looked again at the golden shining carved circular object, bolted onto the side of the pyramid.

"It looks like some kind of old-fashioned seal. Like a seal of office or something."

"That's what it looks like to me too."

"Atlanta, we need to get this info back to my father and Jai to examine."

They snapped gigabytes of photographic evidence and returned to the Rover, relaying them back to Cee-Bee Control. After transmission of the photos, they drove back to the outcrop of basalt columns and bored some core samples from the hard black rock for research back at the lab.

They finished the afternoon's work by collecting as much of the iron pyrites crystals as they could afford to transport within their allotted weight allowance. They also took some test bores at the pyrites field and took some deep cores for lab research. The core samples indicated a lucrative vein of minable pyrites as little as twenty metres below the surface. Jack and Atlanta agreed they would have no problem getting a further Congressional budget for a follow-up project.

Chapter 45

That evening Jai worked at his university lab in the Archaeology Department on the amazingly clear and detailed photos sent back from the Rover. Ewan had stayed with him, although it was not his direct field of study. He remained more for Jai to bounce ideas off, rather than anything else.

"Well, Ewan, I can confirm one thing. The script carved into the circular seal thing is in the same unidentified language as that carved on the red Martian rock in Gary Mackintosh's photos."

"It's a start, Jai, isn't it?"

"Hmm, I guess so. Unlike Gary's red rock, which had Sumerian and Egyptian counterparts to provide rough translations, we don't have a Rosetta Stone to translate this seal. The only positive phrase I can ascertain is here…."

Jai pointed to some carved symbols on one of the photos.

"….That almost certainly says Red Traveller, as it also appears on the other stones. We guess Red Traveller is the name for Mars given by the peoples who devised this language."

"Are we going to need more info to decipher the rest of it?"

"I guess so, Ewan. I'm going to work on the photos through the night. So why don't you head home? We can get back together tomorrow."

With his bad leg playing up from extended sitting, Ewan agreed to call it a night.

Chapter 46

On the following morning, the population of Capitol Base awoke to another of those interminable Martian dust storms, crashing down from the highlands of the Arabia Terra Mountains. Of course, they were protected from the choking dust and violent lightning crashing around the city, outside of their giant super-glass pods.

However, the shift controller at Cee-Bee Control had a problem. The weather disrupted the radio frequencies. He was unable to communicate with the Rover at Base Camp VIII.

*

Jack clicked his radio mic back off.

"Looks like we're incommunicado with Control this morning. They must be having bad weather, solar flaring, or magnetic interference."

Atlanta looked out of the tiny glass pod.

"So far, it looks like another sunny day here. Is the plan to go back to the pyramids and continue researching?"

"No reason not to. Let's keep our eyes peeled for a change in the weather or anything else unexpected."

They drove the Rover back out to the pyrites pyramids. This time, they headed for the middle one of the three, which appeared to be the largest. At its apex, it stood about ten metres above the red dusty surface. As they passed the first pyramid they noticed the Martian wind had almost filled the hole they had dug yesterday. Only the top curve of the circular seal was still visible against the west face.

They chose the west face of the middle pyramid to conduct their dig. No great logical reason apart from this side being the aspect of the pyramid facing directly towards Olympus Mons. Jack and Atlanta's instincts were, whoever constructed these monuments, had an emotional and spiritual connection to the great volcano.

This time they remained in the Rover and used the grab shovels to carefully scrape away larger amounts of the fine dust. This way they were able to reveal more of the west face than yesterday's manual dig at the first pyramid. It did not take them long before they revealed a similar circular seal appended to the face of the gleaming pyramid.

"Start taking photos to send back to Jai. I'll keep digging down, Atlanta."

Atlanta snapped away vigorously with the Rover's camera, simultaneously copying them back to Control for Jai to transcribe. Jack continued to shovel away as carefully as he could, trying not to scrape the side of the pyramid. About half a metre down from the pyramid's seal, Jack spotted something new.

"My God, look at that!"

"More carvings. Do they mean anything to you, Jack?"

They looked like two more seals, although this time the circles were carved directly onto the surface of the pyrites blocks, rather than being appended.

"Atlanta, if I'm not mistaken one of them is written in Sumerian and the other is similar to Egyptian hieroglyphs. We've just found our Rosetta Stone."

Atlanta took dozens of additional photos of the three seals, which were set in a triangular array, symmetrical to the sides of the pyramid. Again, she transmitted copies back for Jai's attention. As Jack prepared to continue carefully excavating, they both felt a sudden shift in the sand below the Rover. It caused the vehicle to settle downwards. Atlanta gave a little start.

"Whoa, careful Jack."

"That wasn't me. But – look at that…."

Jack pointed out through the windscreen. The sand had settled inwards revealing what appeared to be a wide recess, running perpendicular to the sloping pyramid. They both stared in disbelief at the beautifully carved frontage of the recess.

"Jack….that looks to me….like a….a door!"

Chapter 47

Death's-head Moth sat nervously in the restricted room. It was definitely out of bounds for him. He did not have security clearance to be in the room, however, he had kept his eyes and ears open. He learned the key code from a lax and unsuspecting security officer many years ago. No-one had seen fit to change the key code in all these years. Due to its lack of usage, the room was only inspected once a month. Balcanguel was confident he would not be disturbed.

Before joining the priesthood, he had been Space Marine William Balcanguel and he had trained as a weapons specialist. A bit rusty after all these years, but he still had a working knowledge of the S2S-PBA, the space-to-surface particle beam accelerator. Powerful enough to destroy surface-to-air missiles or ground-based armoured vehicles, it would have no difficulty in taking out a small unarmed Rover.

Balcanguel's only problem was he would only get one shot as the MGal3 orbited over the Uranius Patera. He needed to make that call in the next three minutes. He fired up the S2S, which caused the old MGal3 to judder awkwardly in orbit. He also activated the satellite imaging camera.

As the accelerator warmed up, he focussed the surface images on his screen. He sought out the volcano as his initial focal point.

There it is. Uranius Patera.

He zoomed in until he could practically make out every individual rock and gully with perfect clarity.

Two minutes thirty seconds left.

Balcanguel scanned the base of the Patera. He quickly picked out the small glass pod of Base Camp VIII. The Rover was not at the camp. He deduced they must be out on a field trip. Guessing they must have found the pyramids, and if so, he needed to eliminate them.

Two minutes.

Beads of perspiration dotted his brow and upper lip. He knew time was quickly running out. His problem was that he knew about the pyramids, although not their exact location. He started imaging around the base of the volcano until he spotted the pyrites rock field. He must be close.

One minute thirty seconds.

Then he caught the glint of the Martian sun reflecting off the three triangular shapes. Pyramids. He could only hope the Rover was there. MGal3 now orbited directly over the pyramids. His imaging spotted the Rover parked on the west side of the middle structure. Balcanguel could not see any figures outside the vehicle. The S2S's thermal satellite imagery showed two warm bodies still sitting inside.

One minute.

He checked the S2S. It was now fired up to full strength. Time to take the shot. He adjusted the cross-hairs directly onto the roof of the Rover.

*

On the surface, Jack worked furiously clearing the dust away from the 'carved door.' He noticed some sort of protrusion, surrounded by archaic symbols, on the right wall of the sloping recess.

"Look at that, Atlanta? I'm going to give it a prod."

Jack extended his mechanical grab like a closed fist. He tapped the protrusion firmly.

Above them, Balcanguel fired the S2S directly at the Rover. A deadly particle beam shot out of the MGal3, causing the old rust bucket to judder again.

Jack and Atlanta watched open-mouthed as the huge door slid open. This caused the remaining mound of sand they were sitting on to landslide downwards. The Rover slithered down into the gap as if in slow-mo and into the vast void under the golden pyramid.

Behind them, they were rocked by an enormous explosion and flash of light. A huge plume of sand and dust rose into the Martian sky. It also filled the cavernous void with an inky blackness.

*

As the MGal3's orbit pulled away from Uranius Patera, Balcanguel peered through the imaging to determine if he had made the kill. The shot was directly on target. Did he detect some sort of unexpected movement in the Rover before impact? He could not be certain. All he could see was a plume of dust rising above the pyramids as the MGal3 orbited away from the area.

Suddenly, he heard the key code being punched in and the door slid open. Two armed security officers with stun guns held aloft, who had been alerted by the spaceship's juddering, stood staring in disbelief.

"Chaplain – what the hell are you doing in here?"

Chapter 48

The dust storm had passed through Cee-Bee. Radio and satellite links had been restored hours ago. Control had received and transmitted the photos from Atlanta on to Jai and he had been feverishly working on the transcriptions. Six hours later Jai, Ewan, and Jill were sitting in the Oval Office, along with Kurt Reich and Gold sitting pensively behind his desk. Gold coughed nervously, then spoke.

"Before we get to Jai's research, I've got some bad news to impart. Since we received the transmission of the photos this morning, after the radio blackout was lifted, we've been unable to make contact with the Rover."

Ewan replied hesitantly.

"Maybe their radio was damaged by the storm?"

"The storm didn't hit them, Ewan, but, yes, their radio may be on the blink. Possibly Jack and Atlanta may've been hit by something else."

Jill held back tears.

"Something else. What something else?"

Gold nodded to Reich and the Chief of Police took the lead.

"This morning the brother of Blackfriar Balcanguel was detained in the brig aboard the MGal3 space station. Turns out the mild and meek chaplain's a sleeper agent for the Protettorato. William Balcanguel was also an ex-Space marine. He deployed a deadly particle beam and it struck the general locality of the GPS coordinates where...."

Ewan interjected fearfully.

"Where what?"

"....Where the last set of photos were transmitted from."

Jill broke down.

"Oh, my son. These monsters have killed my son."

Gold raised his palms trying to placate the situation.

"Whoa, whoa, whoa! Hold on there, Jill. Kurt didn't say anything about anyone being killed. Control has deployed a long-range drone to get out to these pyramid things and investigate the situation. It'll take another couple of hours to get there. So let's remain calm and wait and see what it finds."

Gold buzzed Juanita to bring in a glass of water for Jill.

"And Juanita, bring in that good bottle of bourbon. Don't know about anyone else here, but I certainly need a stiff drink."

Gold turned to Jai Zhu Pan.

"Okay, Jai, give us what you've got so far."

Jai looked a bit like a rabbit in the headlights. He had never had to give a presentation to a President before. Certainly not one like this.

Chapter 49

Covered in a thick film of red dust, the Rover settled at the bottom of the soil ramp, entombed in the pyramid. Jack and Atlanta could see nothing outside, as the windscreens had been completely covered. A damage limitation check indicated the computer systems were fully-functioning and the lithium cells were eighty percent optimal. The vehicle was still sitting upright with only minor external damage. The mechanical grab Jack used earlier had snapped off as the Rover slid in through the large opening.

The radio was working, however, there was currently no signal in the metallic crystal cavern. They agreed the best option was to don their surface suits and exit the vehicle to assess their overall situation. They had to use the emergency airlock on the roof as the side airlock was jammed with dust piled up against it.

Once outside the Rover, they had to deploy their helmet lights. The cavern was in virtual darkness. The vehicle sat half-buried in the soft, red ramp of dust, close to the smooth flat pyrites floor of the pyramid. They assessed that digging it out would be relatively straightforward.

Their main problem was, the explosion, which they guessed must have been another attack, had blown so much dust in through the door, it had virtually filled the void. Fortunately, they could see a chink of daylight at the top of the dust ramp, about ten metres above the Rover. This gave them something to plan for, in devising an exit strategy.

"Atlanta, I'll start shovelling the dust away from the headlights. You go back in and turn them on. It'll give us better light to work with."

Jack quickly cleared the front of the vehicle. Back inside, Atlanta switched on all the lighting, the headlights, and LED roof lights. The Rover lit up like a Christmas tree and dazzling light reflected around the golden interior of the pyramid.

"Jeez, Atlanta, get back out and see this."

They both stood at the bottom of the slope on the pyrites floor and stared around in amazement. The whole interior, including the walls and the floor, was completely covered in huge intricate carvings, some vividly coloured pictorials, much of it in the indecipherable script. It was reminiscent of photos they had seen at school of the Egyptian tombs built for the Pharaohs.

"Who could have done this, Jack?"

"Whoever or whatever it was, my guess it's a sentient being more advanced than us."

Scanning further around, Jack spotted what looked like a smaller portal on the far sidewall. Jack estimated they had about an hour left in their surface suits before the extreme cold would drive them back into the Rover. He checked the monitor on his sleeve and then rechecked it.

"Atlanta, what temp are you getting?"

She looked at her sleeve monitor in disbelief.

"Mine says 18ºC. Plus 18!"

"So does mine. It's warm in here for some unknown reason, but that gives us more time if we need it."

The air reserves in their backpacks registered just under two and a half hours supply, plenty of time to explore. They strode over to the portal and noticed it had a smaller protrusion on the right side, similar to the larger one Jack had prodded outside the pyramid earlier. He joked half in earnest.

"I'm scared to push the button again. Look what happened last time."

He pressed the protrusion in gently and the portal slid open. They immediately felt a blast of oppressive heat sweeping out through the gap. So much so they had to switch their suits to air-conditioning mode. They both stepped through onto a shiny metallic platform, which had steep metal stairs going down into a deep void. They were about to switch back onto their helmet lights when suddenly the void was lit by an ambient light source. Jack looked around him.

"Must be motion sensors in here and lighting powered by some inbuilt energy source. The platform and stairs look like some kind of galvanised steel alloy. The void has also been carved down through the solid rock."

"Looks like mainly black basalt-type up here, Jack."

"That's what I thought too. Must have taken some digging all this out. Shall we?"

Jack indicated to Atlanta to proceed downwards. Going down the stairs was awkward for them, even though they had railings to hold. The steps were much bigger than treads humans would generally construct. The stairs went down in a zigzag pattern, with a rest platform at each alternate change in direction. By the time they reached the third platform, about thirty metres below the pyramid's floor, they were both perspiring heavily. The atmospheric temperature had risen to 40ºC and the air-con in their suits began to struggle. Jack had a theory.

"We must be reasonably close to a vent from the magma chamber of Uranius Patera. That's where the heat is coming from. It's probably the source of energy providing electricity for the lighting."

Atlanta was concerned.

"Maybe we should head back up to the surface before we cook down here."

Jack looked down into the darkening void. He thought he glimpsed something at the next platform.

"Let's go down one more level. Then we'll return to the Rover. Just keep an eye on your sleeve monitor for temp and air levels."

They struggled down the oversized stairs for about another ten metres until they reached the fourth platform. They shone their helmet lamps at the rock face. The light illuminated a large circular cavity, which disappeared into the inky darkness.

Atlanta let out a fearful scream.

She gripped tightly onto Jack's arm. He was also pretty shaken by the sight. They simultaneously shone their lights onto a skeletal figure sitting propped about a metre inside the cavity. It was certainly of a humanoid form, a giant of a figure, at least 2.5 metres long. The skull had a more bulbous cranium and a more slender and narrower mandible than any homo sapiens.

"This must be one of the beings that constructed all of this. Of course, Atlanta, you know what this means?"

Atlanta was still jittery.

"N - No?"

"It means I'm not the first Martian after all!"

"I'm not in the mood for your sick jokes, Jack. I'm freaking out here as it is."

Atlanta quickly took a few photos of the being. She was becoming exhausted by the heat and frightened by the sight of the alien skeleton.

"Jack, we should get back up soon."

"You're right. But this cavity is here for a reason. Let me grab a couple of samples. Then we'll get back up top."

Jack took a rock-hammer from a side pocket and smashed off a couple of rocks close to the skeleton. He would examine their geological composition later. They began making their exhausting ascent back up to the surface.

Chapter 50

Jack and Atlanta returned to the Rover, spending an hour refreshing themselves from the searing heat down in the void. They had something to eat and drink. Afterward, they did a few basic geological tests on the rock samples. Both concurred on their initial findings, which although highly promising, would require proper testing back in the lab.

After lunch, they agreed Atlanta would start shovelling the dust away from the Rover. Jack would ascend the dust ramp. He would attempt to dig his way out through the narrow gap. The plan, once outside, would be to use his helmet radio and attempt to make contact with Control.

Atlanta began by brushing the thick dust off the Rover's chassis and windscreens. She used a blower attachment to remove the fine particles from the crevices on the chassis and to thoroughly clean the vehicle. She then began the laborious task of shovelling the mounds of red dust piled up around the Rover, so she could drive it down onto the carved pyrites floor of the pyramid.

Meanwhile, Jack struggled to climb up the ten or so metres of the huge soft mound of dust. It was like climbing up a huge dune in the Cydonian desert. He felt like he was treading quicksand. Sometimes the mound would give way beneath him and he would slither back down. However, after about thirty minutes he eventually hauled himself to the chink of daylight coming through the gap at the lintel of the great door.

He shovelled away as carefully as he could removing dust from the gap and widening the opening. He was wary of causing a landslide, undoing all the good work Atlanta was achieving around the Rover. She radioed up to him.

"Jack, I think I've cleared enough. I'm going to see if I can drive the Rover off the dust onto the hard floor."

Jack gave her a thumbs up.

"Copy that."

Jack stopped digging and watched as Atlanta went in through the airlock. He saw the Rover power-up, then Atlanta revved it into gear and slowly drove it forward off the ramp. The rear of the vehicle slightly shunted to the left, then quickly found its grip on the flat surface of the golden pyrites floor. The cavern was so spacious she had enough room to wheel the vehicle around full circle and face the ramp in preparation for a hopeful exit.

"Great stuff, Atlanta."

"Only thing is, Jack. The lithium cells are reduced to forty percent. We must get out of here soon and back to base camp to replenish power."

"Copy that. I'll get back to digging this hole."

Jack now dug away feverishly, sometimes shovelling dust down the ramp and also pushing it out towards the Martian surface. As the gap widened he felt the chill creep into his surface suit. He had to switch off the air-con he had needed in the pyramid back to a thermal boost. The temperature at the gap indicated -23°C. It would only plummet further if and when he got outside the pyramid.

A few minutes later he called Atlanta, still sitting in the Rover.

"I've shifted enough dust. I'm going to try and squeeze out."

"Okay, be careful."

He pushed the shovel out through the gap. Then slowly and carefully he inched his frame out through the narrow opening. He used his arms to continue to paddle dust away from his body, working carefully. He was mindful a tear in his suit would put him in danger.

Finally, he hauled himself out and tried to stand. The dust was ramped downwards on the outside, into the crater caused by the explosion. As he stood up, the dune shifted, giving way under his boots. He tried to grab the side of the pyramid.

The smooth, shiny surface gave him no purchase to grip onto. He began tumbling and rolling downslope.

Atlanta had seen Jack's figure disappear through the gap too quickly, causing her to squeal with fright.

"Jack! Jack! Are you okay?"

After a moment of silence, his voice crackled on the headset, indistinct, but laughing.

"I'm fine, Atlanta. Just had a bit of a rollercoaster ride there."

Chapter 51

Jack was winded. His surface suit was covered in dust, but otherwise, he was unharmed by the tumble. He brushed himself off and prepared to make the radio call to Control. Suddenly, dust started whirling up all around him. It was being whipped up by an object ascending through the Martian atmosphere. Hovering directly above his head. *Were they under attack again?*

His headset crackled into life.

"Control to UCB Rover X. Do you read? Over."

He spotted *UCB Rover X* insignia on the large drone. It landed inside the blast crater. The drone was not here to attack them. It was here to rescue them.

"Jack to Control. Great to see that drone. Over."

On his radio, he could hear loud cheering back in the Control room. His relieved mother came on.

"Jack! Jack! You're alive. I'm so relieved. Is Atlanta okay? Over."

"We're both okay, Mum. Atlanta's in the Rover. It's currently trapped inside the pyramid. We're going to need it hauled out. Over."

Jack switched to his walkie-talkie, letting Atlanta know a rescue was underway. He told her to hold tight.

Jill handed back the mic to the controller. He and Jack discussed a plan to effect a rescue. After agreeing on the best solution, they swung the plan into action. The controller fired an electronic command to the drone. Two steel wires tumbled from its base. On the ends, the reinforced wires had hooks attached, used for transporting equipment.

Jack dragged the first wire up the slope of the blast crater. Heavy, exhausting work, he fed it into the gap downslope, where Atlanta waited at the bottom of the ramp.

"Attach the hook to the Rover's bull bar. I'll get the other one."

Jack returned to the drone, repeating the operation with the other wire. Once the wires were firmly attached to the bull bar, they hauled themselves up the taut wires, until they stood at the gap Jack had widened. Atlanta was relieved at the sight of the rescue drone. They planned to excavate as much of the red dust from the gap as they could manage, to make space for the Rover to exit the pyramid.

Atlanta shovelled away at the top of the slope, making the gap as wide as she could. Jack went downslope a couple of metres on the outside of the crater. He began shovelling out a cavity. His aim was to undermine the side of the crater. He hoped this would cause the top of the crater to collapse, slipping down, and further opening up the gap. There was an inherent risk it would collapse on Jack. He could be buried under tons of red Martian dust.

After about forty-five minutes of exhaustive digging, they were satisfied they had excavated as much as they could tackle. Jack and Atlanta half-strode, half-slipped down the side of the crater. They stepped over to stand close by the drone. Jack radioed the controller.

"UCB Rover X to Control. Commence tightening up the wires. Over."

"Copy that, Jack."

They stood back and watched as the drone slowly rose from the crater. It began hovering backwards, tightening its grip on the steel wires. When the drone was above the third pyramid, the wires had reached maximum tension. They began biting through the top of the slope. The pressure exerted on Jack's undermining efforts worked. The whole top section of the slope gave way. Tons of dust came cascading into the crater. The controller landed the drone back on its original spot.

They waited for the dust to settle and Jack whooped with delight.

"There's a sight to behold."

A huge gap had formed in the pyramid's doorway.

A delighted Jack and Atlanta hugged each other awkwardly in their bulky suits. They returned to the pyramid and back into the Rover. Jack radioed Control to have the drone haul the Rover up and out. He revved the vehicle into gear and waited. As soon as he saw the steel wires tighten, feeling the drag on the Rover, he slowly started driving forward upslope. Edging up to the lip of the large gap, Jack was unsure if the Rover could exit without scraping the top of the lintel. He made a quick call.

"Whoa, Control. Stop pulling for a second. We're not sure if the gap's big enough. Over."

The drone relaxed the tension on the wires. As they pondered on whether to exit for more excavating, they felt the ground shift beneath them. The weight of the Rover was enough to cause the slope to collapse further. The vehicle slithered slowly down a few metres into the crater and freedom.

Chapter 52

By the time they arrived back at Base Camp VIII, darkness rapidly descended. As they parked the Rover beside the camp pod, they spotted Control had transferred the drone from the pyramid to the camp. It had been decided to leave it at the camp meantime until their future situation was resolved. The drone was a freighter-type and not ideal for transporting humans as it did not carry an air supply. In an emergency, using their own air tanks and taking spare tanks from Camp VIII, the drone would be able to carry them back to Camp IV. A backup rescue vehicle could be organised to make it to Camp IV and bring them safely back to Cee-Bee.

However, Jack and Atlanta carried out the tech-checks on the Rover and it showed no computer, technical, or mechanical malfunctions. It had avoided any material damage from the explosion and the unplanned slide down into the pyramid. They would drive back to Cee-Bee as laid down in the project plan. Within a week, they would be back in the city, one day behind schedule.

After a quick dinner, they were both exhausted from the day's exertions, their narrow escape from the attack, and having to dig their way out of the pyramid with the drone's assistance. Jack made a short call to Control, stating they were calling it a night and that they would radio back in the morning. The controller signed off, stating that Jai and Ewan needed to speak with them in the morning.

Chapter 53

After Jack and Atlanta enjoyed a good night's sleep, they were both feeling refreshed. They ate a hearty breakfast, stirred by the invigorating smell of Quorn sausages and reconstituted scrambled eggs, chattering excitedly about returning home to Cee-Bee. Both were keen to complete their research findings on the rock samples and test borings. Jack was itching to start packing up. After changing a couple of depleted lithium batteries and air tanks, they could set off from Camp VIII.

"Atlanta, let's get the call to Control over, then we can get going."

Jack made the call. The controller acknowledged, before passing the mic over to Jai and Ewan. Ewan spoke first.

"Hi, son. You've been through the wars lately. How you both doing? Over."

"Hi, Dad. All I can say is it's been a more frenetic adventure than Atlanta and I had planned for. Over."

"Jack, I'm putting Jai on now. So take care. See you both soon. Over."

Ewan passed the mic to Jai.

"Hey, guys, Jai here. Great to hear you're both safe and sound. It has been quite a trip you have been having. Over."

Jack agreed, adamant they wanted to get home as quickly as possible. Jai agreed to make the call brief. However, before they departed from Base Camp VIII, he wanted to impart some of the findings from his examination of the exciting photos they had transmitted back to Cee-Bee.

Jai discussed the discovery of the giant humanoid skeleton in the underground tunnel. The photos had been examined by an expert anthropologist at UCB, Lucas Kingston. He concluded it was definitely not Homo sapiens. It was also not of any known skeletal hominid-type recorded on Earth. Kingston concluded it was a being that existed on Mars. A Martian!

Without detailed research on the skeleton, including carbon-dating, it was difficult to be precise on the age of the dead being. Kingston estimated it could be somewhere between three million years and a few thousand years old.

"But, don't worry about that, guys. Leave it undisturbed. It will be part of a new research project. Gold has already authorised new funding. Over."

Jai continued. He discussed the photos of the circular pyrites seals above the pyramid doors. In particular, he stated that the seals' scripts in Sumerian and Egyptian hieroglyphs provided a great deal of insight into this ancient Martian culture.

"Jack, these transcriptions were basically what the Protettorato were sworn to protect. They're what they called the Seal of the Revelation. Over."

Jack was stunned.

"Revelation? What revelation?"

Jai outlined the transcriptions detailed that Mars was a dying planet. The planet's atmosphere had been fatally damaged by a giant meteorite strike. Jai stated, from the Martian transcriptions, this was likely to have occurred in the Valles Marineris canyon, gouged out by the meteorite. Life-giving oxygen slowly leaked out of the Martian atmosphere, like air from a balloon with a small pin-prick. All life forms on Mars were slowly dying off.

*

Two or three million years ago, the Martians discovered Earth, their *blue traveller*, contained a viable, breathable atmosphere and they started to visit the blue planet to conduct research. Their plan had been to overtake and repopulate Earth with mass migration from Mars.

The problem the Martians encountered was Earth's gravity. The gravity on Mars was only thirty-eight percent of what Earth once was. If the slender skeletal Martian was atypical at 2.5 metres tall, Lucas Kingston calculated that it weighed about 80 kilograms on Mars, but a crushing 210 kilograms on Earth.

They could not survive on Earth and they were slowly dying on Mars.

The Martians embarked on a programme of transporting samples of Earth's alien life forms back to Mars. A sort of two million-year-old *alien abduction*. Their plan was to mix their genetic DNA with various species, *the last of the great beings of the red traveller sowed his seed among the beings of the blue traveller*. The Martians interbreeding programme had multiple failures, however, among the primate species, they began to have a measure of success.

Jai explained Kingston theorised various transmutations were transplanted back on Earth; Homo erectus, Homo Neanderthalensis, Homo Australopithecus, et cetera. It appears that the Martians successfully interbred and nurtured one particular species, around 2 million years ago. *Many seeds failed. One seed thrived and then there was the new being.*

*

Jack interjected.

"Homo sapiens?"

Jai affirmed Jack's question. Humans were descended from the Martian hominids. They were the *Missing Link*. The Martians kept a close eye on the evolution of Man over many millennia, visiting Earth on many occasions to determine the continued success of their project.

However, life was slowly dying off on their once abundant red planet. It appears that the last visits were made to Earth during the reign of the Egyptian Pharaohs. The last Martians died out around this period. They left behind the transcriptions on their pyrites pyramids, believing that one day Man would venture out into the solar system and discover the origin of their species.

The *Gary Mackintosh* rocks, proof of the Seal of the Revelation, were left on Earth by their Martian progenitors. These rocks were handed down through many generations.

They ended up in the Great Library of Alexandria, then smuggled out of Egypt by the Hebrews. They were eventually passed onto an early orthodox Christian sect, which morphed into the secret Protettorato in mediaeval times.

Atlanta interjected this time.

"Jai, surely the pyrites seals did not convey all that?"

"No, Atlanta, Father Tomek Turkowski has turned state's evidence against his co-accused. He's given the CB Police Department an insight into the inner workings of the Protettorato."

Jai explained the discovery of the Seal of the Revelation was a bombshell to the early Christian sect. It blew much of the theology of the Bible out of the water and, in particular, much of the teachings of the New Testament. This led to the formation of the Protettorato. They were sworn to keep this revelation buried for all eternity.

Jack stated time was pressing. They had to set off for Base Camp VII soon. Jai summed up his findings.

"Jack, there's one other mundane fact carved on the pyrites seals. It lets us know those spectacular golden carved pyramids were not built as tombs for great Martian Kings. They are just...."

Jack replied swiftly.

"Atlanta and I know, Jai. They're *just* ironstone mines. The deep shafts and the ore samples we extracted from the tunnels tell us that. Our research has determined there are still massive iron reserves to be mined. That'll please President Gold. Over."

Epilogue

Jack and Atlanta made it safely back to Capitol Base within the week, entering by the Western Airlock to a rapturous welcoming crowd. After the usual obligatory speech-making, they were much happier returning to their geological research at UCB. Their samples and borings revealed more than just extensive iron ore deposits. Significant traces of other metals and minerals had been discovered; including, lead, tin, copper, sulphur, silica, diamond, and quartz. Uranius Patera had revealed multiple untapped resources. The expectation was, this was just the beginning of a new era.

Using state aid, with the Government taking a fifty percent stake, Jack and Atlanta set up a new mining company. Three Pyramids Mining. Jack Sinclair was elected as CEO and Atlanta Caie elected as Director, Research & Development. Kurt Reich was appointed as part-time non-executive Director of Security. The plan was to begin extracting iron ore by mid-2113.

Jack and Atlanta were married on 22 June 2112 at St Andrew's Church, in the presence of their proud parents, friends, and family. They were even graced by the presence of President Elijah Gold and his First Lady attending the wedding as guests of honour.

Gold's ratings had soared with the success of the UCB Rover X project, the solving of the Joe Jaap murder, and the dismantling of the secret sect of the Protettorato. He was re-elected in November 2112 for a second term as President on a ticket of bold economic expansion. Kurt Reich was also successfully re-elected as Chief of Police.

In the autumn of 2112, Jack Sinclair, Jai Zhu Pan, and Lucas Kingston secured funding for an extensive revisiting of the Three Pyramid mining site at Uranius Patera. Using four Rovers and travelling via the restocked and extended Base Camps, they carried out geological, archaeological, and anthropological research at the golden pyrites pyramids.

Jack's research determined that the vertical shafts and horizontal tunnels excavated by the Martians many millennia ago were relatively structurally intact. New winding gears, lift shafts and air-conditioning units would have to be constructed and installed before full-scale mining production could begin in 2113. A new miners' camp would have to be erected near the pyramids. Experienced ice miners were queuing up to apply for the new and better-paid employment opportunities.

Lucas Kingston's research on the original Martian skeletal remains discovered by Jack and Atlanta, and others discovered in the tunnels on the second expedition, revealed that the Martian race became extinct about 2000 BCE. The earliest bones discovered were carbon-dated to around two million years old, revealing a race of hominids, equally, if not more, intelligent and advanced than the humans now currently living on Mars.

Jai's research on the intricate carvings and writings on the well-preserved inner walls of the pyramids revealed much of the lives and culture of the Martian race. They called themselves the Bor-ak. The Bor-ak had developed into an advanced technological race, having developed space travel within the solar system. They were a peace-loving people, having eradicated war and strife over many past millennia.

The Bor-ak were also fervently religious people. They worshipped the Sun for its life-giving properties, however, in general, they believed in an omnipotent creator god, named Vor. Their god Vor lived in the heavens of Vor-maga. Vor-maga was the Bor-ak name for Olympus Mons, a truly sacred place for the Martian people.

Jai was uncertain on the timeframe detailing exactly when the meteorite struck the Valles Marineris, as the carved pyrites scripts became quite sketchy after this point. It appears that this region of Mars, where the main cities lay, included the capital Khor-Ek-Kada. Huge swathes of the Bor-ak population were wiped out instantly by the nuclear blast caused by the meteorite impact. Oceans and seas were evaporated and the red planet began its slow and painful death.

Much of the Martian script then concentrated on the need to save the Bor-ak gene pool by transmutation with the less evolved Earth-bound hominids. Homo sapiens, the smaller cousins of the Bor-ak, became their success story. The script remained unfinished around 2000 BCE, but it described a final spacecraft leaving the red planet to check out the continued evolutionary development of Man. It appeared to suggest the spacecraft also contained the seeds of the Bor-ak, their Martian DNA, which would slingshot around the Sun and be blasted out of the solar system into deep space. The pyrites script ended at this juncture, but Jai assumed this mission was in the hope that one day the Martian DNA would find a new, habitable planet somewhere out in the vast Milky Way galaxy.

Ewan continued his work as Emeritus Professor of Astrophysics at UCB. He was now majoring in research for Earth-type planets orbiting in the Goldilocks zones of their parent stars. Jill still fronted her breakfast show *Good Morning Mars* until she went on maternity leave. She gave birth to a healthy, bouncing baby girl named Jayne Geeson Sinclair on 3 November 2112.

About the author

Derek Beaugarde is a pseudonym for his fictional science fiction publications and Derek Niven is used by the author John McGee, a member of ASGRA, for his factual genealogical sports publications. John McGee, aka *The Two Dereks*, was born in 1956 in the railway village of Corkerhill, Glasgow. He attended Mosspark Primary and Allan Glen's schools. The late, great actor Sir Dirk Bogarde spent two unhappy years at Allan Glen's when he was a pupil named Derek Niven van den Bogaerde. The observant reader will readily discern the origin of the two pseudonyms. After spending 34 years in the rail industry in train planning and accountancy, John McGee retired in 2007. In 2012, the idea for his apocalyptic science fiction novel first emerged, and 2084 The End of Days © Derek Beaugarde was published by Corkerhill Press in 2016. This was followed by Pride of the Lions © Derek Niven published in 2017, Pride of the Jocks © Derek Niven, foreword by Kathleen Murdoch, published in 2018, Pride of the Bears © Derek Niven published in 2020 and Pride of the Hearts © Derek Niven published in 2021.

Other Books in the 2084 Trilogy
by Derek Beaugarde